PENGUIN BOOKS

THE CAGE

Andrea Newman was born in Dover in 1938 and brought up in Shropshire and Cheshire. In 1960 she graduated from London University, where she married while still a student, and then worked as a civil servant and a teacher before becoming a full-time writer.

Her publications include *A Share of the World* (1964), *Mirage* (1965), *Three into Two Won't Go* (1967), *Alexa* (1968), *A Bouquet of Barbed Wire* (1969), *An Evil Streak* (1977), and *Another Bouquet* ... (1978). *A Bouquet of Barbed Wire* was dramatized by her for London Weekend Television, and *Another Bouquet* ... followed in early 1977. She has also contributed to other television series such as *Tales of Unease*, *The Frighteners*, *Love Story*, *Seven Faces of Woman*, *Intimate Strangers* and *Helen, A Woman of Today*.

Andrea Newman is divorced and lives in London.

D0529916

ANDREA NEWMAN

THE CAGE

PENGUIN BOOKS

Penguin Books Ltd, Harmondsworth, Middlesex, England
Penguin Books, 625 Madison Avenue, New York, New York 10022, U.S.A.
Penguin Books Australia Ltd, Ringwood, Victoria, Australia
Penguin Books Canada Ltd, 2801 John Street, Markham, Ontario, Canada L3R 1B4
Penguin Books (N.Z.) Ltd, 182–190 Wairau Road, Auckland 10, New Zealand

—

First published in Great Britain by Anthony Blond 1966
Published in Penguin Books 1978

—

Copyright © Andrea Newman, 1965, 1966
All rights reserved

—

Made and printed in Great Britain by
C. Nicholls & Company Ltd
Set in Linotype Juliana

PART 1

ONE

IT was like joining a gloomy secret society. It cut through all barriers of nationality and class; even the centuries became meaningless. I felt myself instantly in touch with all women who had ever lived and experienced this terror. Currently the last in line, I joined the long, wretched queue. We were like those cut-out paper dolls that children play with. I could sense their fingertips touching mine; I was almost conscious of their reminiscent sympathy.

I didn't tell anyone. I, who had never been superstitious, suddenly became a creature ruled by taboos. To put my fears into words would give them reality. As long as I was silent, as long as I admitted nothing, there might be nothing to admit. And so I split my mind in half, resolutely laughing at my own absurdity while I kept ceaseless, panic-stricken watch. The half that was watching must not be caught watching by the half that knew there was nothing to worry about. As anyone else's problem it would have been comic.

The days passed and I reverted to childhood magic. I placed my shoes neatly side by side under the bed and knew I would wake with the reassuring pain. If I could take three dessert spoons out of the drawer without looking, and not get them muddled with the soup spoons, all would be well. I was even reduced to cracks in the pavement and counting to a lucky number before someone spoke. And all the time, just as frantically, I despised myself, not only because the magic was useless but because I didn't need magic anyway.

There were times when I didn't think about it at all: when I was asleep, of course, although sleeping became increasingly difficult, but also at quite ordinary times during the day when we were busy in the shop or I was at home watching television. I would behave quite normally for a while, even (which was more important to me) *think* normally; then I would have to remember and immediately everything went into reverse, minus signs for plus. The most trivial thing could have this effect – planning a winter coat, for instance.

Sometimes I thought there were hopeful symptoms but I could never be sure I hadn't imagined them. I tried all ways of relaxing in order to sneak up on myself and find out how I really felt. I prayed a lot; it was years since I had put such feeling into prayer, not since I promised God that I'd be good for ever if only he'd make Daddy not be dead.

At work and at home I had to exercise really savage discipline to stop myself rushing off to the lavatory every ten minutes. Almost as soon as I left it I had this impression that something marvellous had happened and if only I could run back there I'd find that everything was all right. It never was.

I even tried common sense. I put it off because it involved thinking back in some detail, but eventually I tried it. I thought over our precautions, which had seemed adequate at the time and had been adequate before. Did I really have cause to worry? Then my mind, too outraged to concentrate, slid off the subject and returned to the lavatory, the prayers, the magic.

The one thing I never dared to do was look at my university acceptance letter again. It lay as always in my dressing-table drawer and my fingers brushed the handle and stroked the wood while I gazed out of the window and refused to believe...

Everything became grotesque. I was two people: my normal self and this hunted animal. It was hideous that the answer, one way or the other, was actually in me and I didn't know what it was. It was like being blindfolded: was there really something waiting to pounce or was I alone in the room?

I didn't cry, though, and I didn't panic, quite, though it

was a near thing once or twice. I think it was the feeling of helplessness that brought me closest to panic: I had always been in such excellent control of my own life. It was vital this should continue; it seemed the only proof of my identity. Whatever happened (and I still couldn't use the words) there must be some decision only I could make.

I suppose on the whole I was pretty uncommunicative at home. My mother, luckily, assumed I was pining for Malcolm. She brought in his two postcards with such obvious pleasure: something to cheer me up at last. I had to be very cheered. It was actually a shock to be reminded of his existence. People who depend on physical magnetism don't seem to stay alive very well in the mind; I had noticed this before, even with girls. But the postcards were evidence: he *was* alive and on holiday, having a good time but looking forward to seeing me again. And he – it seemed ironic somehow – would have to be the first to know; if there was anything to know.

Saturday, then, was my deadline.

TWO

HE came into the shop where I stood bashing the cash register in quiet despair. All hint or pretence of symptoms had gone; since Thursday I had become so fatalistic that I had abandoned all supernatural aid, divine or home-grown. Yet I still caught my breath when I saw him. He tanned easily, being so dark, and the holiday weather had been kind. He was wearing fawn slacks and a bright blue shirt and he looked – well, good enough to remind me how I had got into this situation in the first place. I needed reminding.

He smiled and I managed to smile back; then he came over to the till, the far side, away from the customers. I went on mechanically pressing buttons; I was glad to have something to do.

Malcolm said, 'Hullo, slave.'

I said, 'Hullo,' pressed the button for total and gave a woman change from a five pound note. 'Had a good time?' I added.

'Great. Something lacking, though; d'you know what I mean?'

'I can guess.' I humped great tins of fruit out of a basket and clicked up our special offer price over and over again. I had even forgotten the line in sexy, humorous banter that Malcolm and I used, presumably to cover the absence of what did not exist. But I still spoke it without thought, like someone relapsing into a foreign language used many years ago.

'You doing anything tonight?' he was asking.

I pretended, automatically, to concentrate. 'No, I don't think so.'

'Must be my lucky day. Shall we go to the Drome then?'

Our local dance-hall was still called the Drome by everyone who remembered it in its days as a cinema called the Picturedrome. It now had a smart new name that nobody bothered to use. The very thought of it, with its seething clients shoving each other all over the floor and occasionally departing upstairs to the cinema seats for necking sessions, or something more ambitious in an empty passage or the deserted car-park, suddenly and perhaps for the first time revolted me. I went on fishing in the depths of the wire basket for Oxo cubes that had got loose from their packet. 'Can't we just go for a drive?' I said.

I felt, rather than saw, him look pleased. He probably imagined he could read my mind. It was almost amusing. 'Good idea,' he said casually. 'We can have a meal somewhere. Look, you'll be through here in half an hour. Shall I hang on and run you home?'

It was all so normal and there had been so many Saturdays like it. There was, of course, no absolute reason why this one should be different. It was up to me : if I could act well enough to survive an enthusiastic reunion there was no need to say anything yet, or perhaps ever. But I did not really believe this.

'Okay,' I said, 'but hang on outside. You'll get me the sack.'

He leaned forward and looked at me closely for a moment. 'Are you all right?' he said. 'You look a bit pale.'

There was a lull between customers, but it was hardly the place for a moment of truth. 'Who doesn't, next to you?' I said.

'Yeah, it's not bad.' He was pleased. He eyed me speculatively. 'D'you like it?'

I looked away. 'Yes, it suits you.'

'Okay, baby.' He strolled round to the other side of the till, doing his pseudo-American. 'I'll take a pack of cigarettes.' He was chewing hard on imaginary gum. He flung down his money and it rolled around in mad little circles, flattening itself.

I gave him the cigarettes and the best I could do lately by way of a smile. 'Look, you'll get me shot,' I said. Customers were lining up behind him. 'I'll see you outside in half an hour.'

THREE

As a child I used to have this fantasy that until something actually happened it was avoidable. If I was due somewhere at nine o'clock, say, I was not certain to be late, no matter how far away I was, until nine o'clock actually struck. Similarly on visits to the dentist I could postpone the shock impact: until he actually put the drill in my mouth he might not be going to put the drill in my mouth. So now, with Malcolm. I had a vital, beautiful half-hour in which anything (meaning only one thing) might happen and save me. No, two: I could be lucky and be granted the lesser miracle of having the world come to an end.

When at last all the customers had gone and the shop was closed I cashed up very slowly and carefully. It balanced near enough; I could never understand why it was hardly ever exact. I was sure I always gave the right change and I checked the float first thing in the morning. I wished now that it took longer to cash up. I was too conscious of Malcolm waiting outside; I felt like a murderer about to drop my bomb on his expectations of a nice, cosy, sexy evening like all the others, only better after a fortnight's separation.

Mr Mackenzie was conscious of him, too. 'You run along,' he said, winking at me. 'Don't want to keep the boy-friend waiting.'

I took refuge in the cloakroom, repaired my face and brushed my hair. I felt very alone. My face in the mirror looked at me anxiously. 'Chin up, kid,' I said to it. 'I won't desert you.'

Malcolm was pacing a trifle impatiently. 'You don't hurry,

do you?' he said. 'Still, you're worth waiting for,' he added as though I was arguing.

It was only a ten-minute drive and I kept him busy talking about Jeff who had gone with him on holiday. At home I changed while he talked to Mother, who liked him. Everything was happening much too fast. Very soon I was back in the car and we were setting off for the country. Malcolm squeezed my hand and lingered over the knee it rested on. 'Damn these light evenings,' he said. 'Where would you like to eat?'

I took cigarettes and matches and lit up for both of us.

'Just get out of the village and park somewhere quiet,' I said. 'I want to talk to you.'

'That sounds ominous.' He speeded up as we got clear of traffic. His voice was oddly neutral. 'Are you going to give me the boot?'

'No, of course not,' I said. 'Why should I?' I looked at the scenery flashing past us and thought I could always hurl myself out. That was one solution.

'Well, you didn't look all that thrilled to see me just now. You could have . . . met someone else while I was away.'

'So could you.'

'Yes, I could.' He sounded doubtful. 'But I haven't.'

'Well, neither have I,' I said. I felt humbled; it had never occurred to me that he might have met someone else.

'Just as well. I bought you a record. Sinatra. It's in my suitcase.'

'I thought you might,' I said. 'That's why I'm still here.'

I swear if we'd crashed the car and lain in the road bleeding to death we'd still have talked like this. We talked Lancashire, Cockney, American, or a blend of all three; we played it cool, casual, hot-blooded, or a paper-back mixture; we saw films and went to jazz concerts and drove too fast and discussed these pastimes. But we never had what I'd call a conversation. I don't just mean something serious and heavy, but the sort of talk where you really say what you mean and make discoveries about yourself and each other and get closer together. The sort of conversation you have late at night with a really good friend. I tried once or twice, before I found out that Malcolm only *looked* like my ideal man, but it never worked. It didn't even fail spectacularly ('What the hell are you talking about?') but merely limped to its death in a platitude ('People are funny,' or maybe: 'That's the way it goes,' or even, joking: 'I'd never have thought of it like that. You can tell I left school at sixteen.'). The real humility behind this made me angry sometimes. But he went on being amusing and thoughtful and generous; above all, he went on being attractive ... oh God. When you meet someone who really looks every inch, but exactly, what you've always wanted, you can't not go out with him. And when you find, as you feared, that he's not the one who's waiting for you somewhere and who'll be so great it won't matter what he looks like, should you give him up on the instant?

I knew the answer really: you can go on seeing him, of course; just don't go too far. It's so easy for them, people giving this advice; they're not going out with someone who knocks them senseless with excitement and whom everyone else is running after. I don't know how much of it is vanity: it is hard at eighteen, nineteen, to resist when you can get someone everyone wants and he only wants you. And you have such sublime confidence in yourself and your ability to handle a situation, any situation. Perhaps this very confidence lets you slide further than you intended. I can't even speak for other girls. Plenty of them manage to avoid this situation, certainly, and parents and magazines all warn you against the desires of young men. But nobody ever warned me against myself.

'Okay, baby, let's have it.' Malcolm had stopped the car.

I turned my head; I wanted to face him, rather like a firing squad. 'There's a slight chance I'm pregnant,' I said.

FOUR

HE took it well. I was watching for panic, but there was no sign of it. Shock, yes, which was only to be expected.

'But you can't be.'

A strictly conventional reaction, like saying, 'Oh no,' when you're told someone's dead. At least on television.

'I know,' I said, 'but I'm ten days overdue all the same. You know it was due three days after you left. Well, it just never came. And it still hasn't.'

He put out a hand to me, but I pretended not to understand and passed him the cigarettes instead. I could not have endured contact just then. We both had cigarettes.

'Don't worry,' he said, then added, 'Sorry, that's a bloody stupid remark. I just mean we mustn't panic.'

'Who's panicking?'

'Oh, I'm sorry.' He looked really upset. 'You've had this on your own for ten days. God, I wish I'd had a fixed address; you could have written.'

'I wouldn't have,' I said.

'Why ever not?'

'Well, it could have been a false alarm and I'd have worried you for nothing. I kept thinking it would come.' I couldn't remember now what I had thought; it seemed that I had been living in this state for ever.

'Yes, of course.' He frowned. 'I suppose there's still a chance that it might.'

'Yes, there's still a chance,' I said.

'But you don't think it will?'

'No.'

The word said itself. I had not fully realized the extent of my own pessimism. There was a silence.

'Right, then,' said Malcolm. 'We must act on the assumption that it won't.'

I was alarmed, even angry. 'What d'you mean, act?'

He stared at me, then past me. 'Well, make plans.'

There was something about his tone that scared me sick. I wanted passionately to contradict myself. 'Don't be silly,' I said. 'I was just being fatalistic. It's still only a possibility. I'm often two or three days late; you know I am. It's really only a week overdue. That may not mean anything.'

Malcolm said evenly, 'And has it ever happened before?'

I almost screamed at him. 'Don't be so eager.'

'Val, I'm not being eager; of course I'm not. I just want to face facts.'

'Well, I don't.' I shook in my seat.

'All right then,' he said stiffly. 'What do you suggest?'

Everything rose up in me. I was hot and cold; my eyes burned and my throat ached. 'Oh Christ,' I said, shocking myself, 'I just want to be dead.'

I felt so violent I could have killed him or killed myself or got out of the car and run till I dropped. Instead I just cried. At first I pushed him away very roughly when he tried to put his arm round me, but later I turned and cried on his shoulder, soaking the blue shirt. He stroked my hair and said nothing. Presently I sat up and groped for a mirror in my bag.

'I've ruined my face,' I said unsteadily. 'And they call this waterproof mascara.' I got to work with a tissue. 'My eyeliner's all over the place, too. I shall have to take the whole lot off and start again.' It was a relief to look in the mirror, even at such a horrible sight; my own face gave me moral support.

'Val.' His voice was very quiet and serious. 'I'm sorry, love.'

It calmed and sobered me. 'I know,' I said. 'So am I.'

'If it has happened,' he went on cautiously, 'I don't know how because I was careful, honestly.'

'I know you were,' I said.

'It could have been that time I didn't have anything with me and I just ... you know,' he said, embarrassed. 'But I was careful. Maybe I left it too late but I thought it was all right. All the other times –'

I interrupted. 'Yes, I know. Maybe it's true what they say about making some with holes in.' My tears had washed away a lot of feeling. 'It's funny really, isn't it? We thought we were being so clever. We couldn't understand why people took risks. Anyway, it may be all right. I really don't know. I just thought I should warn you. I couldn't have managed to pretend everything was all right in any case.'

'No, of course not.' He lit fresh cigarettes for us. 'Have you told anyone else?'

'No. There's only Marianne I could tell and I haven't got her new address. She hasn't rung up for ages; you know how elusive she is.'

'You couldn't talk to Sally?'

'No.' I couldn't have looked Sally, with her prudence and her engagement ring, in the face. 'Anyway, aren't you *glad* I haven't told anyone?'

'Yes. Yes, of course. I just meant it might have helped to talk to someone ... well, to Marianne, if she was around.'

'Well, she wasn't. And I don't think I really wanted to tell anyone. I didn't want to talk about it.'

He was frowning. 'How about your mother? Will she have noticed anything?'

'Well, it's a bit soon for that.'

'No, I mean that you're late.'

'Oh, I see. No, I don't think so. I don't announce it every month.' It was a startling thought and one that should have occurred to me. 'It'd be different if I suffered a lot. God, I hope she hasn't noticed.'

18

'I don't expect she has.'

'Well, you thought of it.'

'It was an idea – forget it.'

'How can I forget it?'

'Oh Val, I'm sorry. You know what I mean. It was just a silly idea.'

I tried to be rational. 'I don't think she has really. She was all cheerful when she brought your postcards in.'

'That's okay then.'

I went on working at my face. Malcolm threw away his cigarette and lit another. There was a pause, a slightly uncomfortable one. We had not really said anything of importance yet. I did not want to, but I felt the weight of all we had not said. I shut my bag with a click.

'Well,' I said, 'there you are. I just thought I'd mention it. Shall we drive on?'

He turned to look at me. He seemed shocked. 'But there's a lot to discuss,' he said. 'Isn't there?'

I studied his face, still just the same after my little explosion. Superb. Thick eyebrows, nose a little crooked from some football accident, the only asymmetrical feature and probably an asset, mouth rather more lush than was expected in a man, but the general build and toughness left you in no doubt. Yes, a winning face all right. A pity he was so much less than his face.

'Is there?' I said. 'Let's not rush our fences.'

'I'm not rushing anything.' (I could feel him being patient with me, wary.) 'If everything's all right, well, fine; we can forget what we said. But if it isn't we'll have to talk some time, won't we?'

He was being perfectly reasonable. But inside me something was writhing and twisting in all directions to avoid facing the unspeakable. I did not want to put it into words.

'Could it be some other time?' I said.

He stared at me. I could feel his reluctance and it rather

19

surprised me. He seemed more ready to face the situation than I had expected. 'I just want you to know where I stand. I'm right here with you. I feel very responsible.'

'No,' I said. 'It's my own fault.'

'Well, you couldn't have got in this situation alone. Obviously we share the blame.'

'No,' I said. 'I had more at stake than you. Look – can we leave it? Just not discuss it any more. I can't stand it. Let's just drop the subject till we really know for sure one way or the other. All right?'

He looked away. 'When will that be?'

I tried to remember what I had read in women's magazines in the far-off days when the subject had been merely interesting. 'I think you can have some kind of test with animals when you're a fortnight late.'

'The middle of next week then?'

'Yes.'

'Your half-day?'

'I suppose so. I'd have to go into town – I couldn't risk it here.'

'No, of course not.' He hesitated. 'D'you want me to come? I could try to get off work early.'

'Don't be ridiculous,' I said. 'You've only just got back from holiday. I'm perfectly capable of getting on a bus with a bottle in my handbag.'

'Bottle?'

'Urine,' I said, sharply and cruelly.

'Oh, sorry.'

'Don't be sorry. Easier than blood-doning. Let's just hope my mother doesn't ask questions or try to come with me. I really need an excuse: Marianne would be ideal but my mother knows I haven't got her address.'

'The library,' he said simply.

'Oh yes.' I was terribly angry; I could feel myself shaking. 'How very clever of you. That will do splendidly.' I looked around me and began to understand the expression 'blind with rage'. 'And now do you think we could have something to eat? I'm rather hungry.'

He started the car, but we didn't move off. Instead he turned his head as though about to say something. I went on staring in front of me. He sighed, or swore, very softly and we moved away.

We didn't talk. On our way to the restaurant we passed Mrs Franklin out for a walk with her husband. I had forgotten she lived round there. She waved, so I had to wave back, and smile.

It was just four months since I had left school.

FIVE

MRS Franklin shook me warmly by the hand. 'I won't say good-bye,' she said, 'because I hope you'll come to see us from time to time, either before you go or during the vac.'

'I certainly will,' I said. I felt awkward, grateful, embarrassed. We had worked so hard together for so long and now it was over: achieved. 'I want to thank you for all you've done,' I added.

'Nonsense; I've enjoyed it,' she said briskly. 'I'm only sorry we didn't quite make Oxford. But never mind. The train service is better from London.'

We smiled at each other.

'All the same,' she went on, 'don't come up too often. Three years is a long time and you don't want to get too serious about that boy-friend of yours.'

'Don't worry,' I said. 'There's no chance of that.'

Leaving anywhere is sad, however glad you are to go. I got through the day pretty well, but no credit to me: as head girl I was busy with end-of-term duties. One moment caught me unprepared, though. In the English book-room I paused for a moment, looking through the window at the spring sunshine on the tennis courts and the movements and voices of the Juniors playing, and the moment crystallized, quite alarmingly, into something both trivial and significant that I knew I would always remember. Until then I had not known what would represent my eight years at this school and now it was fixed. Not a form-room, not the library, not a person, but this.

The other bad time was during assembly, as I had expected. Handing in my badge and being applauded was easy, but the music nearly demoralized me. Some schools use *God Be in my Head* regularly, and so provide immunity. Ours played it only at the end of term and my nerves were raw. When all the work and the duties and the occasional resentment end, you forget so quickly. Boredom fades and sentiment takes over. I looked round the hall at the dark wood panelling and the neat uniformed backs of the girls in front, and the music went slowly on, flooding me with affection for everyone and everything. I was laughing at myself and fighting the tears simultaneously.

Jean was a great help. She was waiting in the playground when I came from seeing Miss Lloyd, and we walked down the path together as usual. Her satchel and shoebag were overflowing; her gym-shoes hung round her neck.

'You've been ages,' she said accusingly.

'I know,' I said. 'Sorry.'

'It's all right.' She sighed. 'Gosh, you are lucky. Fancy having *left*.'

I said lightly, 'Well, if I'd stayed much longer I'd have qualified for a pension.'

She ignored that. 'I wish I could leave.'

'Jeanie, we've been into all that.'

'I can leave in fifteen months.' She peered at me. 'Legally. Can't I?'

'Yes, you can,' I said, very casual: big sister trying to be clever. 'But you'd be a fool if you did.'

'Why?'

'Because there's not much point in going to a grammar school if you don't take any exams at the end of it and you've no idea what you want to do. If you leave at fifteen you'll go into some dead-end job and then maybe you'll want to do something else and you won't have the qualifications. You could spoil your whole life like that.' God, I felt pompous and elderly, but I did mean it.

'I'm not clever like you.' She said it very matter-of-factly. 'And I bet I get married young, anyway.'

I wanted to laugh, but it would have hurt her feelings. 'Quite possibly,' I said, 'but you can't tell yet and anyway it's best to be on the safe side. Even if you do, you may still need a job and it's better to have one you enjoy. You shouldn't close doors on yourself.'

Then I stopped listening properly while Jean painted an elaborate picture of herself as the wife of a millionaire. We were walking down the hill towards the bus station and the usual wind was blowing. I scarcely remembered the town without a wind. Sometimes it blew the scent of the gas-works in your face. In the mornings after getting off the bus I walked to school behind young girls who wore no stockings with their high-heeled shoes and whose feet looked pale and dirty. It was possible that they were very happy in the factory, but I didn't want Jean to be one of them. At least, not unless she really wanted to be, I always added to myself, but it was not strictly true. I felt we were all worthy of better things: Mother, Jean and I. It was too late for Mother, but I wanted Jean to be as lucky as I was and to find her own escape route.

'Can I open my report and say you let me?' she was asking, the routine end-of-term question.

I gave the routine answer she expected. 'No, you can't,' and took it out of her hands. She pouted and sulked, playing the game to the end, as reassured as I was that our *status quo* existed. She was very much my kid sister and if she'd run into the road I'd have flung myself under the bus automatically.

SIX

YES, you could call us a close-knit family. It had something to do with Mother being a widow. I'd been grown-up as long as I could remember and we'd discussed young Jean, and whether we could afford a holiday, and what colour to have the house repainted. Somehow this meant Jean and I couldn't be friends. It was more than the five years between us, though that could have been enough. But Mother and I were the adults, taking care of her. So Jean and I just had this terrific affection, nothing more. We weren't on the same side.

I didn't feel lonely or deprived or anything. I knew I'd have someone for me one day, just as Mother had had Daddy, until he died. She always talked to me a lot about him and how happy they'd been, more as I grew older, until I wasn't sure how much I remembered, how much I had been told. I felt very privileged when we had these conversations, yet at the same time it all seemed quite normal and nothing special to get excited about. I didn't envy girls at school who had fathers alive because I knew they were inferior to my dead one.

The parents of my friends at school reinforced this conviction. Sally's parents gushed, but you never felt they meant a word of it. Marianne's parents ignored me, just as they ignored Marianne. Her mother had run off with, of all music-hall jokes, a commercial traveller, when Marianne was ten, and her stepmother took this to mean that only repressive discipline would save Marianne from a similar end. When she wasn't doing her duty in this respect she was busy turning her grocer's shop into a gold-mine. Marianne's father helped her with both enterprises, but in a weak kind of way, like a man who has been proved wrong so often he knows better than to risk an opinion again. None of this mattered to me, as a visitor, but it must have been pretty rough as a permanent state. I always used to go home and hug Mother extra hard after visits and she'd say, 'They can't be as bad as all that,' and I'd say, 'They are.' I wouldn't have blamed them as much if they'd got drunk or gambled or done something positive. But when Marianne went from twenty-second to fifteenth in her form they never even noticed, and when Sally made a dress she could actually get into, her parents got so excited you'd have thought they'd given birth to Dior. Whereas I had my terrific mother to come home to, always there with a cup of tea and (after I was seventeen) a cigarette for me, and ready to talk or listen, whatever the day demanded, or even to let me go and closet myself upstairs because she understood or remembered that sometimes you didn't want anyone, and sometimes you didn't even mind being unhappy.

She had a job in a dress shop in the village and they used to let her go half an hour early so she could be home before us. She must have read all the magazines; she had this thing about her children not coming home to an empty house. Actually, I did appreciate it. It was lucky for her, of course, that the school was a half-hour's bus journey away and I so frequently stayed for games practice or rehearsals and always made Jean wait for me. I was hardly ever home before five o'clock, often later.

I didn't find school tiring, though; I used to wonder what all those sentimental articles in the newspapers were about. Everyone seemed so upset to think of kids in school having to work. Yet there was no other way to get what you wanted, and after sixteen you were only working at what interested you, anyway.

I did eight 'O' levels, then three 'A' levels and scholarship and entrance to Oxford and Cambridge, who, as it turned out, didn't want me, and London, who did. It was hard work, but there was a purpose, so it wasn't tiring. I 'played a full part', as they say, in the life of the school. I was form captain five times. I was captain of tennis, netball and swimming teams on various occasions. I did a lot of acting and wrote articles for the school magazine. I was a prefect as soon as I could have been, and because I didn't care who hated me, few people did.

I had it all taped; I was so well organized. I had to have a good-looking boy-friend, too, with a car, the sort that makes people envious. For a year it only got me into pleasant situations and I never let it interfere with my work. Malcolm used to complain that I wouldn't go out with him often enough. It was a question of priorities and I never had any trouble deciding. I knew what I wanted; I had been working for it all my life.

So now, whatever happened, I would blame no one but myself. I wouldn't have it any other way.

SEVEN

THE test was positive, as I had known it would be. I had to ring up for the result. They had warned me that this was not absolutely conclusive, just almost, but I knew anyway. I think I had really only had the test to stop Malcolm from making plans for another week. This respite seemed important. After I had made the phone-call I should have rung Malcolm but I didn't; I just went and sat in the park for the rest of my lunch-hour and looked at the kids swinging and sliding down the chute and jumping on and off the roundabout as it moved. Further down was the pavilion where courting couples could shelter on wet nights and where Malcolm and I had often made love when it was dark and empty. Beyond that were bushes and hedges that provided cover when the pavilion was occupied. These weren't our only places; the car gave us mobility and the woods were full of quiet spots if you didn't mind the insects and an occasional invasion of boy scouts. There was even the car itself, in a cramped kind of way. It had never seemed sordid, any of it, just exciting and, after quite a short while, necessary. To each his own addiction.

Was I really so abnormal? Was I 'that kind of girl', to be avoided in the street for fear of contamination? I had never thought of myself or Marianne in those terms, but there were plenty who would. The clichés multiplied : did we have bad blood, where did we go wrong?

I was 'normal', I suppose, at twelve, when Marianne was being slapped by her stepmother for wearing lipstick and staying out late, and boys to me were just creatures to be beaten in class and in sport. I was intensely competitive and had only

28

recently left my co-ed school to go to what the village called 'the girls' grammar'. I was equipped with basic knowledge of the so-called facts of life, soberly acquired from my mother and augmented gradually in biology lessons, wider reading and whispered consultations with Marianne who acquired unlikely and somehow squalid information about douches and tablets and lavatory seats, never anything straight forward, so that our education was largely complementary. I was normal at fourteen, too, when after restreaming I saw more of Sally who was still in my form and who giggled at everything; and we went to school dances and were clumsily kissed by fifteen-year-old boys alongside the bicycle sheds but fled if their hands started to wander. Whereas Marianne had already advanced to the heavy petting that made her popular and left her cold, and I nearly lost my good name for ever when I beat up the girl who said, 'Marianne Hart, the well-known tart'. She thought she was brilliantly clever but at least had enough sense to keep her mouth as tightly shut as mine when we were both hauled up before the headmistress. Janet's friends consoled her and Marianne mopped me up, repeating all the time, 'Val, you shouldn't have, honest,' but she was crying, just the same, as she pushed her thick, dyed hair out of her eyes. And she said – pathetically, illogically, I don't know, but it moved me a great deal – 'I can't be a tart, Val; I don't even enjoy it.'

So when did I start on my corrupt path that would make welfare workers click their tongues over me? Soon afterwards, presumably, at about fifteen when with kissing perfected and necking so thoroughly explored that it had become just plain exhausting, I first discovered real sensation. So far Sally and I had romped in the comparative safety of group activity where 'Lights Out' did not entail the orgy it suggested. All casual stuff that left parents content as we went around with the gang. Then we started to pair off, to go steady, for weeks or months at a time as everyone in our form was doing, and it was the fashion to pretend to have gone further than you really had but most important not to go too far, and we evolved codes and numbers and letters, all kinds of symbols, to indicate to each other, without reaching crude detail, what stage we were at. I went out with Les and I was fond of him because he was tough and casual and nearly eighteen, so I let his hands go further than anyone else's had, and was shocked by the strength of my own response. Was this what Marianne did not enjoy?

I sensed danger and part of me wanted to retreat. Like a scientist discovering a secret weapon I feared I was unleashing something I might be unable to control. But Les was persistent, after such a promising start, and some of me was on his side. I slid back, after token resistance, and sensation enveloped me again, immeasurably stronger but still unmistakably from the same source as those vague stirrings I had had for years when reading love scenes, watching film idols or starting to smoke in secret.

I now saw the point of Sally's waistline restriction, which made her into a kind of toll-gate, the charge being an engagement ring. I talked to Sally and she deplored my lack of wisdom and left me in no doubt about the stages immediately before me if I allowed Les to continue unchecked. I controlled my unsuitable reaction to this and made further efforts to restrain Les. These scenes, starting with an argument, always seemed to end in a repetition of what I was trying (or partly trying) to avoid. So, unable to reform Les, but not without regret, I gave him up. I was left with the far more serious problem of trying to reform myself.

For a while I tried to play the field again. But the field had thinned out into pairs. Luckily I was saved (at sixteen) by exams, which I always regarded as more important than anything. I put up with a feeling of vague dissatisfaction and diverted my energies to work. For several months I added almost uninterrupted work to a basis of pretty steady application. My results were what you would expect.

That summer I went to France with Sally and her parents,

and while she flirted and giggled with everyone in sight I met Michel, who was slight and dark and beautiful and spoke very little English, and launched myself rapidly into a supercharged repetition of the Les episode. I knew what I was doing, but because we were only there for two weeks I told myself it didn't matter. I would never have moved so fast in England, but the language problem seemed to make it all excusable. It was a wonderful release, pure joy, like taking a bath after a desert trek. I didn't feel wicked at all, just ecstatic. From Michel, too, I learned to pay a little unselfish attention to my partner. I became all-powerful.

Back home I exercised this power over successive boy-friends. I still seemed a reassuring distance from anything risky even though I had not stuck to Sally's commandments. I may have been swayed by the fact that Marianne had already at fifteen abandoned our conviction that whatever else was allowed, actual virginity must be preserved. This belief was rigidly held in our group, although our jokes suggested otherwise. I never forgot the shock and amazement we all felt when we euphemistically discussed her lapses. We were alarmed; she had stepped over the boundary and gone from us. When I talked to her she did not seem to know why she had done it. 'It doesn't seem important. I don't know – it's not worth arguing over. It's so important to them and it doesn't mean a thing to me.' She wasn't in love with any of them but she always felt something : affection, interest, admiration, gratitude. She collected more presents than any girl I ever heard of outside fiction, but the turnover in escorts was rapid. I was afraid for her, but she herself was unworried; unthinking, even. She left school at sixteen with poor results; she had never been academic and the preceding two years had been crowded with boy-friends and rows at home. She went into an office, was terribly shocked when the married boss made a pass at her, left, tried shops, then shuttled between shops and offices for a year. Sally had gone into hairdressing and I was left alone with the comparatively straitlaced majority of my form. It didn't worry me unduly; I had a lot of work to do.

Marianne envied me gently. 'You *are* lucky, Val; you've always known what you wanted to do.' She was bored at work and unhappy at home; she enjoyed herself only when she was taken out. 'You see, I don't know what I want to do. If I did, I'd do it.' She gave her open, childish grin. I always felt very old and protective with her. Then came the grand, final showdown : she either walked or was thrown out. I never knew all the details. She was a pale, ill-looking waif for weeks after, living in town in a variety of bed-sitting rooms, trying to be a model but generally out of work. She'd get behind with rent and have to move on at speed. It was really rather shattering to see someone you knew well going downhill like that. She used to come to us for week-ends occasionally and my mother made a fuss of her and was all ready to go and plead for her with her parents, but Marianne said she'd rather die than go back. She had a way of making clichés sound fresh; she said them as if she didn't know they were clichés.

Then we were all eighteen and Sally was going steady with Bill and saving up to get engaged, and I was packing up without regret boy-friends who impeded my final sprint towards 'A' level, and Marianne met David Kemp. She'd begun to make a small success of her modelling : she had started to look cleaner and arrive on time, have some of the abundant curl taken out of her long, thick hair and tone down the strawberry colour somewhat, get some decent pictures taken. Anyway, she met David. He was supposed to be a reporter on a local paper, but his father virtually owned it and David seemed to work only when it suited him. He had beautiful clothes and a brand-new sports car and money to lash around, but none of this influenced Marianne. She just fell in love with him. She fell harder than I'd imagined it possible for a human being to fall. Everything became subordinated to David : work, friends, everything. She organized her life around him and would refuse any job if there was the merest possibility that he might even telephone that day. For a while she even talked of literally nothing but David. His attentions were very spasmodic, and in between meetings she just died a few hundred times. She spent whatever money she had on making herself look beautiful for him, and after a while it seemed he must be paying her rent because she moved to quite a nice flat where she stayed whether working or not, for some time, until David went abroad for three months and she started moving around again. But she never went out with anyone else. It looked so serious that I asked if she intended to marry him, but she said simply, 'I'm not good enough for him.'

It was to Marianne that I went that evening when I should have been telling Malcolm the test result. She had phoned me the day before with her new address and I arranged to see her although I knew Malcolm expected me to meet him. I rang up and left a message for him, very discreet. I didn't want to see him. I wanted to go to ground, to bury myself. Normally this would have meant solitude, as it had done all through my adolescence, but I was a little too strained for that : I wanted softness and comfort.

Marianne never let me down provided I kept her in proper focus between visits. Now when we met she was wearing a pink cardigan, rather grubby, and black trews. She was far too feminine for them. Her hair was all over the place, very curly and long, and the dye was growing out. Behind the too heavy make-up her face looked very young.

'Val.' She hugged me with the desperate, drowning strength she always used whether happy or sad. 'It's marvellous to see you.' She held me away from her for examination. 'Your hair's marvellous – all shiny and swinging. But you do look a bit washed out. Are you all right, love? You sounded ever so depressed on the phone. Come upstairs; I'll make you a cup of tea.'

She led the way. She was living in one of her awful places

again, all dust and cats and cabbage. I wondered if I could move in and never be seen or heard of again.

In the immensely crowded bed-sitter she stepped over débris to put on the kettle, then took another look at me. 'Val, what is it?' she said. 'You're not all right.'

I sat down and lit a cigarette. 'No, I'm pregnant,' I said. Even the second time round it still sounded absurdly melodramatic. I hated it.

Marianne just looked at me, for nearly a full minute, in silence. Then she said what I had not allowed Malcolm to say, what I had tried to shut away even from myself: 'Oh Val, and you were going to college.'

EIGHT

MARIANNE'S kettle was screaming. I must have been silent for some time. The small windows were open, but the room was still stuffy. From outside came the yells of kids playing in the streets.

I said, 'Yes,' and Marianne took off the kettle. It was as though she could not move until I answered her. I went on, 'There must be a way I can still get there. They've accepted me – I've got the letter.' My voice shook. 'Marianne, what am I going to do?'

'Are you quite sure?'

I nodded. 'I've had a test.'

'Oh.'

We were both mute again. Doors banged and one tenant shouted a message to another up the stairs.

'Does Malcolm know?' Marianne said finally.

'Yes. Well, not the result of the test, I only got that today, but he knew there wasn't much hope.'

'How did he take it?'

'Oh, he took it well.' I tried to muffle the scorn or whatever it was that gave such an edge to my voice.

Marianne said very gently, 'You're not in love with him, are you?'

'No.'

'Not at all?'

'No.' I felt the need to justify myself. 'We've had a lot of fun together, going to places, and he's terribly attractive; I'm quite fond of him in a way, or I *was*, till this happened. I can't exactly feel affection at the moment. But that's all.'

I stopped. It had always felt all right as a point of view, inside me. But it sounded terrible.

Marianne said, to my surprise, 'It's like you were the wrong way round.'

'What?'

She looked apologetic. 'It's like you were the boy and he was the girl. I mean in your feelings about each other.'

'Oh no,' I said quickly, 'he's not in love with me either. We've both just been having a good time.'

'But if he's taking it well – ' she hesitated – 'maybe he's not as upset as you, maybe he didn't want you to go away or something.'

'You mean he did it on purpose so I'd stay at home?' I said, angry.

'Oh no, no. Oh dear, I'm saying all the wrong things.' She pushed back her hair and again put on the kettle which had been peacefully cooling. 'Look, Val, never mind me. I'm up the creek. What are you going to do? Is there anything I can do to help?'

'I don't know,' I said. 'I don't seem to be able to think. It's not just Malcolm and me, even; there's Mother and Jean, and everyone in the village. I know one shouldn't mind what people say, but it's such a small place.'

'I know.' She looked uncomfortable at the memory. 'It was bad enough at home and it wasn't all that small. They'd gossip over nothing.'

There was a pause. Then I said bravely, perhaps defiantly, 'Well, I can't go to the university this October, if I'm pregnant. Maybe they'll take me next year.'

Marianne looked at me. 'But how can you ...' she said, and stopped.

'I've got to get there,' I said. 'I can't let this ruin my whole life. People do go away and have babies and get them adopted and nobody ever finds out.'

'You mean – just walk out and not tell your mother *anything*?'

'Well,' I said, 'it's one possibility.'

Marianne made tea. 'You couldn't do it,' she said. 'With my stepmother, yes. But not with a mother like yours. You couldn't.'

I sighed and shut my eyes. 'No, you're right; I couldn't,' I said, 'though God knows it might be the kindest thing for all concerned in the end.'

Marianne shook her head. 'Your mother'd go mad with worry,' she said.

'Well, she won't be exactly thrilled if I tell her the truth.'

'I know. But can you imagine – if you just walked out and she never heard anything?'

We drank tea and looked at the carpet.

'Okay,' I said at last. 'You're right. At least, I don't know if you're right but I see your point. I'm just working through the possibilities. That's one we've ruled out.'

'Of course,' Marianne said in a small voice, 'the most obvious one is getting married.'

'It's not Leap year.'

'Oh please.' She looked shocked. 'Don't joke about it.'

'For God's sake, if I can't joke about it, who can?'

'I know. I'm sorry.'

I started pacing around. 'Look – in circumstances like these, *particularly* in circumstances like these, it is nicer to be asked.'

'Don't you think he'll ask you?'

'Yes, I think he probably will.' I stopped moving. That must have been one thing I had worked so hard to avoid last week. 'I think that's what I'm afraid of. I'm afraid I won't have the strength to say no.'

'Must you say no?'

'Look, Marianne, you just don't marry someone who is dead sexy and quite pleasant and nothing more. That is not enough for a lifetime. It's not marriage and it's not what I want.' I didn't know why I was so vehement; no one could force me to get married. 'I'll give you an example. When

I needed an excuse to go into town for the test, Malcolm suggested the library. He doesn't even realize what the library means to me. He's *that* insensitive. He laughed at my university reading list and said, "Do you really have to read all those books?" He used to get quite annoyed when I was working instead of going out with him. He even wanted me to go to university in town, when Mrs Franklin was putting me in for Oxford and London. He doesn't understand.'

Marianne looked sad. She said, 'You want a superman.'

'Yes, I do. You're quite right. It's possible; people do it. My mother did it. That's what I want.'

She nodded. She looked so patient and self-effacing that I suddenly felt remorseful. 'Oh Marianne, I'm sorry. Let's talk about you. Is David back yet?'

Her face cleared slightly, but she answered in a halting way as if half her mind was still on me. 'Not till next week. That's why I'm living here. He gave me some money before he went and I'm trying to make it last for clothes and things. I've been working in a shop again; I only just chucked it. I've got to go to the hairdresser and that.'

'What are you going to have done?'

'I'm not sure really.' She was talking very slowly, almost unwillingly. 'Last time I went they said I mustn't have it dyed and straightened and I'm not sure which I want most.'

'How does David like it?'

'Oh, I don't really know – Val, I can't keep this up, I'm sorry. What are you going to do? I've not been any help.' She hesitated. 'D'you want me to try and find someone who could – do something? I could ask David next week.' She blushed slightly. 'He might know.'

I stared at her. This was something I had not considered. Abortion, like suicide, seemed a solution for other people. 'I'm not sure,' I said slowly.

'The only thing is,' Marianne said, looking at me, 'it might be expensive. But – look, Val, don't be offended, please – I've got the money David left me and I don't really need it, I mean I'd be glad – '

'That's sweet of you,' I said, unnerved by the way in which we were sheltering from the enormity of the thing behind a wall of finance. 'But I've got a bit from my job anyway. Only – ' I paused. Faced with a really practical solution I found it hard to explain my reluctance. I had no ethical objections, certainly; I did not regard the thing inside me as a person. 'I don't think I could,' I said feebly.

'No.' Marianne seemed relieved. 'It's – ' But she broke off, and from the look on her face I expected to hear her say 'murder' at least. 'Awfully risky,' she said after a long pause.

'Yes.' It was simpler to agree with her. But it was not fear that I felt, rather the enormous obscenity of entrusting my body, so trained and cherished, to alien hands, and this was something too private to express.

'There are pills, of course,' she said. 'You're supposed to take them as quickly as possible, as soon as you're late. But they don't always work.' She paused. 'They make you feel ever so funny. Sort of . . . far away.'

The whole conversation alarmed me; I wondered how far it was based on experience and the idea made me cold. 'Well, I don't suppose I'd notice that,' I said lightly. 'I feel pretty remote already.'

Marianne was frowning. 'Only thing is, I can't get them till next week when David gets back and I think that's too late.' She looked guilty, as if she were responsible for my state. 'I'm sorry, Val. I'm not being any help.'

'Forget it,' I said. There was a certain doomed inevitability about the whole thing which seemed appropriate. 'They might do some awful damage anyway.' I was trying to be cheerful, to remove the stricken look from her face.

'I didn't want to take them,' she said slowly, almost apologetically. 'But David said I had to. I think they're quite safe. He said they were.'

'I should hope so.' I felt indignant that although Marianne

had left home she was still being pushed around with no one to protect her. And yet Sally, for instance, found life so smooth. 'You want to be careful,' I said inadequately. I was not sure even now that I had heard the whole story; and not at all sure that I wanted to.

'I know.' She looked humble as she had at school when told not to do whatever it was: wear nail varnish, forget homework, skip games. The look deceived some people, at first anyway, but her behaviour never changed. I gave up.

'I'd better go,' I said. 'I've got a lot of thinking to do before I see Malcolm tomorrow.'

NINE

MALCOLM was angry, and like most angry people he overdid it. 'Don't I have a right to know what's going on?' he demanded loudly.

'Oh sure,' I said. I was very tired; I had hardly slept at all.

'You can see Marianne any time. I was just as concerned as you were about the result. Why the hell couldn't you let me know yesterday?'

I closed my eyes. 'Because I'm selfish and inconsiderate, probably.'

He tried again. 'I know Marianne is your friend, but this is important. We have things to talk about.'

'I know,' I said. 'That's why I went to see Marianne. I wanted some peace.'

'What d'you mean?'

'Peace. You know. And quiet. I didn't feel like talking.'

'But we've got to talk.' He seemed baffled.

'I know,' I said. My eyes were still shut. Perhaps sudden and permanent blindness would make the whole thing less painful. 'Talk away,' I said.

There was the silence I expected, then I heard him light a cigarette. The scent of the smoke was very keen. Perhaps it really was true about loss of one sense making the others sharper.

'I've been doing a lot of thinking,' he said eventually.

'You too,' I murmured.

He went on as if he had not heard me. 'And I think we ought to get married.'

I had to open my eyes. 'That's great,' I said. 'What

a splendid sense of duty you have. So you're going to do the decent thing. Well, it takes two to tango, and I'm not playing.' My metaphors were a little mixed, but the general drift was clear enough.

'I'm sorry,' he said. 'I put it badly. I want you to marry me.'

'You're proposing.'

'Yes.' He was not looking at me.

'Well, I think it's very brave of you. After all, for all you know, I might accept.'

'I want you to.'

'Oh, careful. You sound as if you mean it.'

'I do mean it.' He turned to face me. 'Shut up and listen a minute, Val. I wanted to say this before we knew for sure, before you had a test or anything, but you wouldn't let me. Sure, I was shocked at first, when you told me. I thought we were in the clear. But these things happen. We've had a great time but we've never talked about getting married. That's because you were going away. But this changes everything. I'd always thought I'd still see you when you were home on holiday and maybe we'd write, and then when you'd finished college, if we hadn't met anyone else, either of us, we might sort of pick up where we left off.'

He stopped. I didn't say anything; I felt cold all over.

He added, 'Well, it's just happened sooner, that's all.'

'Not quite,' I said.

His mouth tightened. 'No, not quite. It's mucked up your going to college and I know what that means to you. Believe me, I'm sorry. But it's not the end of the world. You can still read books – all the books you want. You've always said how important that is. You can go to night school if you like.'

'Yes,' I said, 'I can do all that.'

'You see,' he went on, 'it needn't be so bad. Look Val, the way I see it, if we don't get married, how are we going to feel, knowing we have a child and we're not together? If you stayed at home with it, I'd be seeing you both every day; I'd go mad. And if you had it adopted – well, could you ever stop wondering where it was and if it was all right? I don't think I could.'

'You seem to be a born father,' I said.

'Well, don't you feel like that?'

'No,' I said. 'I don't feel anything.'

'You will,' he said reassuringly. 'You're still upset. Look, I'm not pushing you for an answer now. But I think we can make a go of it. Don't you? We've had a lot of good times together.'

'I know,' I said, 'but that's not enough. Is it? Do you really think it is?'

'I think if we try it could be. Oh, I know we didn't plan it like this, either of us, but that's the way it goes. I wasn't just out for what I could get, you know that. Anyone'd be proud to go out with you, you're so gorgeous. Oh Val – ' his voice changed – 'why are you sitting so far away? Mum and Dad won't be home for hours.' He moved closer.

'What, now?' I said. But I already felt excited where I had never expected to feel anything again.

'Why not? It can't do any harm. We haven't really said hullo since I got back. Maybe I can persuade you to marry me.' He went on soft-talking while he started to warm me up.

He was much more familiar in this role, stronger and more attractive. Besides, I had read somewhere that this could bring on a miscarriage. But mainly, I think, I just wanted him, though I had thought I never would again. On top of me he looked so powerful, watching me and saying, 'That's it, you're doing fine. That's my girl,' and I could shut my eyes and float away up to the top, soaring on that indescribable pleasure that you somehow forget almost as soon as it ends, but I opened my eyes in time to see his face, that intensely private look of pain and joy, all given to me, and I wished to God I loved him.

'There, that didn't hurt, did it?' He was always flippant afterwards.

'No,' I said. 'You haven't lost your touch.'

'No more skulking in the bushes and waiting for parents to go out if we get married,' he said, holding my hand.

'I'll be fat,' I said.

'It doesn't matter.'

I felt very warm and relaxed, though I still knew with my mind that marriage should be more than this.

'I'll have cravings,' I said.

'Maybe I can satisfy them.'

'For strange foods.'

'Oh well, we'll manage.'

'On your salary?'

'I shall rob the bank.'

'Well, you couldn't be nearer.'

We laughed. It all seemed much too easy. What was I doing?

'Are we engaged then?' he asked suddenly.

I felt threatened again. 'You said you wouldn't rush me.'

'Okay, but I want to buy you a ring.'

I shook my head. 'I don't want one.'

'But I want you to have one.'

'No. They're for people who meant to get married anyway.'

'Don't go on about it,' he said. He sounded embarrassed.

'All right. But you promised to let me think. I want to think. Will you let me?'

'Okay.' He seemed reluctant. 'But don't be too long. It's not very flattering.'

I felt a sudden wave of guilt and kissed him very hard. He was pleased and surprised. 'I'll tell you tomorrow,' I said.

TEN

IT'S funny how you still play for time when it can't do you any good. I did, anyway. It was Sunday and I went up into the hills by myself. Malcolm had put the alternatives before me very clearly, but I still had this final reluctance to put my head into the noose.

It was Mother and Jean, really. Mother never interfered or asked questions, so I didn't know how she thought I felt about him, but I did know that there wasn't any way to explain how I became pregnant without being in love. She had talked to me about sex in marriage but always with the stress on love. She talked, presumably, as it had been for her. If I was pregnant, I must love Malcolm; if I loved Malcolm I must want to marry him. Unless some miracle happened, that was the way she would think and I was damned lucky she wasn't the sort of mother who would just think the whole thing was plain disgusting.

She wasn't to know that when she talked to me of Daddy I'd pictured someone I'd meet one day who would look like Malcolm, perhaps, but have read all the books in the world and know about things I'd never even heard of. He'd teach me so much that I'd admire him till I nearly burst. We'd be very close, but however hard I tried I'd never quite beat him at anything and he'd always take terrific care of me. We'd turn day into night until we could read each other's thoughts and we'd discover things – oh, I don't know – but wonderful things, like islands where no one had ever been before. We wouldn't work at ordinary jobs, we'd always be off somewhere exciting and time wouldn't mean a thing. If we had children it would be when we wanted them and they wouldn't spoil anything. We'd still sail round the world.

The tears ran all down my face and on to my shirt because I hardly noticed them. I'd never told anyone my dream; I'd been saving it up for him. Other people would have laughed, but to me it was a solid dream, not castles in Spain. To lose it was to break faith. I was giving up something real.

My shirt was cold and damp. I blew my nose and tried to calm myself. Jean. Supposing even that Mother understood and forgave me, how did I explain to Jean? She adored Malcolm; she thought the whole thing was terribly romantic. I was responsible for her. If I didn't get married, if I had the baby and stayed at home, would she think it was all right to behave like that? Or would she despise me for what I had done? The five years between us were a lifetime and I had not let her down yet.

I tried to attack myself from all angles. Were my motives really so pure? Wasn't I plain scared of the people in the village watching me bulge out of my coat? Gossip, simple gossip: just words, to frighten me. And my pride: no longer Valerie Ayden, snob, going to university, but Valerie Ayden, unmarried mother. Was I strong enough for that?

It was a drab day and the hills were quiet; not many people were out. I had seen this view many times and it seemed a mockery that it looked the same when my life was so changed. I wanted to hold on to the grass and the earth to give me strength. I wanted to stay there for ever where no one could inquire or demand anything.

Was it Mother and Jean, or the village? I don't know. But I didn't stand a chance.

ELEVEN

WE waited until Jean had gone to bed. I made Malcolm go out for cigarettes because I wanted to tell Mother alone. He was very reluctant. We sat in the kitchen and argued.

'She's my mother and I want to tell her.'

'But we're in this together.'

'All right, but I've let her down, not you. I want to tell her alone. Can't you see that?'

'You're shutting me out, Val.'

'No, it's the relationship we have.' I could feel my precarious strength ebbing. 'For God's sake, Malcolm, just give me ten minutes.'

He went. I must have looked as desperate as I felt. Presently I lit a cigarette and went into the sitting-room. She was watching television and she looked very small. It was enough that Daddy had died and now I was about to do this to her.

'I heard the door,' she said. 'Has Malcolm gone early?'

'Only for cigarettes.' My voice sounded very strange to me. I had to go straight on or I would have run away. 'I made him go out because I've got something to tell you and I'm so ashamed I don't know how to say it.'

She looked at me, alarmed, and my eyes told her. I might have known she'd somehow spare me the words. I nodded.

'Oh, my child.' She never called me that. Her voice didn't sound normal, either. She got up very quickly and put her arms around me, but I had cried so much on the hills I couldn't cry any more. 'Don't worry,' she said, 'you've told me now.

Sit down.' We both sat on the couch. The television continued, madly cheerful.

'I'm sorry,' I said. 'I'm terribly sorry.'

'Hush.' She rocked me and I felt ten years old. 'I know you're sorry.'

The front door banged. It was not ten minutes, only five. I got up, but my mother held my hand. Malcolm came in and looked at us both.

'Has Val told you, Mrs Ayden?' he asked.

My mother said, 'Yes.'

'I'm awfully sorry,' he said. 'It's all my fault. I want you to know that.'

'No,' I said sharply.

My mother ignored us both. She was looking at the television set. 'Malcolm, please turn that thing off for me,' she said, 'and then would you mind putting the kettle on? We'll have some tea while we talk.'

I suppose if we'd heard we had four minutes until the Bomb we'd have rushed for the kettle. The more enormous the event, the more trivial your response to it. Malcolm went into the kitchen and we waited for him to come back.

'You should have told me before,' my mother said. 'As soon as you were afraid. If I can't help you now, what am I for?'

I looked at her and felt my eyes burning. 'How is it you always find the right thing to say?' I wanted to go on but I couldn't.

Malcolm came back. He looked too young to be in this mess. I pitied him. I felt very calm and generous and about a hundred years old.

'We want to get married,' he said.

I held my breath. My mother said, 'Yes,' in a way that could have meant anything.

'As soon as possible,' Malcolm added.

My mother sighed. I could feel her looking at us both. 'It's not quite as simple as that.'

Malcolm rushed on. 'Oh, I know we have to ask your permission as Val's only nineteen, but you will give it, won't you? I mean, there's no point in wasting time, is there?'

'Well,' said my mother after a pause, 'a quick wedding won't hide the fact that Valerie is pregnant.' (It cut through me to hear her say the word.) 'It will only draw attention to it. I think we should all realize that people are going to talk anyway, and then forget it. We should only do what is best for you and Valerie and the baby.'

'That's what we want to do,' Malcolm said. 'Surely getting married quickly is best for me and Val and the baby?'

'If you're really sure.'

'We're sure,' I said.

My mother lit a cigarette and passed us the box. 'I think in this situation there's a risk of rushing into marriage because you only feel conscious of the urgency. And marriage is too serious and important to be rushed into, ever.'

'Oh, we've thought about it a lot,' Malcolm said.

I could feel my mother's affection for him and yet I knew she was surprised we had ever come to this.

'I realize how you feel about each other,' she said slowly, 'although I never thought it was so serious. I thought you both knew how much work you had to do first.' She hesitated. 'I may seem calm, but that doesn't mean this hasn't been a shock.'

I couldn't speak at all. Malcolm said, 'Oh, we realize that. We're very sorry.'

My mother went on as if there had been no interruption. 'Valerie had so much ahead of her; this is going to cut right across her education. And you, Malcolm, you won't find the money that keeps you nicely at home will go very far when you have a wife and child to support.'

'We know that,' Malcolm said in a low voice.

'I had to say it,' my mother continued. 'There's no point in pretending that getting married will solve everything. It can never be as easy as it would have been if you had waited. I want you to be very clear about what you are taking on. Because there is a choice. Valerie can stay here and have the baby and you can still see each other, and if you're still sure you want to get married when there's no urgency, you can do so with my blessing. I'm trying to help you, not make you feel worse, believe me.'

She meant so well; she couldn't know it was far too late for all this sweet reason. I felt sick at the thought of reopening the debate I had held with myself for the past week. There was only one deal I could accept and that she couldn't offer me: to take the baby off my hands and let me go to university. She had her living to earn and young Jean to support and there was nearly a year now before I could re-apply. She couldn't look after the baby and she wouldn't want me to give it away. I wondered if she had any idea what it was to me: not a person but an embarrassing encumbrance that was going to spoil my life. I hoped not. But if I stayed at home she would certainly find out. Perhaps more of our actions than we know are governed by a desire to be well thought of. Rather a humiliating discovery.

'Do your parents know, Malcolm?' my mother asked suddenly.

He shook his head. 'Not yet.'

'Would you like me to tell them?' Really there was no limit to her generosity.

'No,' said Malcolm. 'It's my job.'

I saw her look at him with respect and I was envious. 'Yes, it is really.'

'I'll tell them tonight,' Malcolm said, 'as soon as I get in.'

I had not thought about Malcolm's parents' role in this at all. I had always felt so superior to them. Well, I was certainly cut down to size now, dependent on their goodwill not to look, not to speak, not to behave in a certain way. His father, coarse and smart, the kind of man once referred to as dapper, and his mother, who talked about nothing in a loud voice as if it mattered. And yet these were details. There

50

was no end to the punishment once it started. You got on the roller-coaster without realizing and you were on for the whole ride.

'In that case,' said my mother, 'would you tell them I'd like to see them tomorrow?'

'Yes, of course,' Malcolm said. They were suddenly in charge of the whole thing. I was superfluous.

Tea was made and we drank it and smoked more cigarettes.

'I'm very grateful, Mrs Ayden,' Malcolm said. 'You've been wonderful.'

My mother looked at him and then at her cup. 'Well,' she said, 'There's no point in lecturing you both. You know what you've done. I can't help by reminding you.'

'You mustn't worry,' Malcolm said earnestly. 'I'll be a good husband to Val.'

My mother said slowly, 'Yes, I expect you will. But could we talk about that tomorrow? I'm very tired now and I'd like to be alone with Valerie.'

'Of course.' He stood up, suddenly looking embarrassed.

'Good night,' I said. 'I'll see you tomorrow.'

'Yes.' He hesitated, then started to move. 'I'll be going, then. Good night, Mrs Ayden.' He stopped in the doorway and I was afraid he was going to thank her again, but he didn't.

When he had gone I felt the space in the room like a physical weight. I had never been so alone with my mother. She looked years older, and exhausted. She said eventually, 'Are you really sure what you want to do?' and I could see that speech was an enormous effort for her. It was probably many years since she had felt my father's absence so keenly.

I said, 'Yes, I'm sure.'

She put out her cigarette and lit another, a thing I had never seen her do before. 'He's a nice boy,' she said. 'But it's much too soon. In three years, when you were qualified, if you still felt the same . . .'

I said, 'Yes, I know'. It was like slowly bleeding to death.

She said, almost to herself, 'I should have realized.'

'No. *Please.*' Intolerable that she should blame herself.

She looked at me and I wanted to fling myself on her and howl and clutch at her. 'I want you to be happy,' she said.

'I will be.'

She smiled faintly. 'It won't be easy,' she said, 'however much you love each other. When things are difficult you'll have to fight the temptation to blame each other, to say cruel things. You mustn't ever do that. It's so destructive.'

I nodded. There was a silence while she seemed to gather strength. 'Marriage can be wonderful,' she said, 'but it's very hard work. It's the only really full-time job there is. You have to work so hard just to keep what you have and even harder to make it grow. But it's more rewarding than any-thing else. If you really feel ready for all that with Malcolm, then I'll give my permission gladly. But I had to say this to you.'

She had said many similar things before but never with so much feeling and memory. I made a supreme effort; I couldn't let her down.

'Thank you for saying it.' My voice shook very slightly. 'And I am ready.'

She got up and I knew that neither of us dared to risk a good night kiss. 'Sleep well,' she said.

TWELVE

OUR whole relationship was subtly altered. We were, if anything, closer, but it was no longer carefree. Our emotion, however, had reached its peak and was now deflected into action. There was so much to do. My mother saw everyone who had to be seen before I did, shielding me with her whole self. The family doctor was kind and business-like. The vicar kept his homily to a minimum. People in the village tried to look at me normally. Malcolm's parents made grandiose gestures of acceptance.

She wrote to the university for me. And she told Jean.

At first we didn't talk about it. Jean circled round me, trying to start, while I watched, too scared to help her. About two days after Mother had told her, she came into my room.

'Can I be your bridesmaid?' she asked.

I said, 'Of course you can,' and waited. She ran a finger round the edge of my dressing-table. I wanted to hug her but it would have given the moment too great importance.

'I'm *glad* you're going to marry Malcolm,' she said finally. 'I think it's ever so romantic.'

'Well...' I was desperately feeling my way. 'It would have been more romantic if we'd waited longer.'

'Oh ...' She went on stroking the wood. 'Mother did tell me.' She said (carefully repeating a lesson) 'she didn't want me not to know anything other people know. I – I'll be an aunt, won't I?'

'Yes.'

'And Malcolm will be my brother-in-law.'

'That's right.'

She hesitated. 'Can I come and see you a lot?'

'Yes, of course. All the time.'

She looked up. You could almost see her shedding a load. She lifted something from the dressing-table. 'Can I practise with your eye-liner?'

I stopped feeling. I had a very complete sensation of having burned my boats and yet in some corner of my mind there was an escape clause which I refused to examine. It sustained me.

I spent what energy I had on preparations. I left my job, gladly, though I should have to find another one after the wedding. While Malcolm worked I looked for flats. Near home they were expensive, growing cheaper though more dismal nearer town. I wanted to be as far as possible from everyone I knew.

'You know you'd be welcome to live with us,' said Malcolm's mother. 'We've not much room but we don't mind squashing up a bit. You'd be all right in Malcolm's old room, at least till the baby comes.' She made it sound like a sinister space visitor.

'I know,' I said, careful and polite, 'but I think we ought to find our own place really, for everyone's sake. Thank you all the same.'

'Well, it's your life.' She eyed me suspiciously. 'I know your mother feels that way.' I could see her wondering what I, so hide-bound by my mother, was going to do to her darling son once I had taken him away from her protection.

Most landladies specified no children, no animals, rather in the style of 'no hawkers, no circulars', which I had seen on gates in the village. Many of them also said no coloured. They prefaced all these prohibitions with the word 'sorry'. I had never had occasion to notice any of this before. Now the words leaped at me from the ad columns of the papers. I had joined a select company of unwanted tenants.

There seemed no point in pretending to landladies that I wasn't pregnant and then being thrown out the moment I started to bulge, so I wore the ring Malcolm had already bought me (plain, gold and very narrow by my choice) and called myself Mrs Ross. I said our present flat was too small now that I was expecting a baby.

'You're very young, dear, aren't you?' said one old thing who gave new meaning to the word crone.

'Yes,' I said. It was the simplest answer.

'You young people,' she said, 'getting married earlier and earlier these days.'

I said nothing. She peered at me. 'Well, I don't know,' she said. 'I'd like to help you. What does your husband do, dear?'

'He works in a bank.'

'Does he now? Well, that's quite respectable, isn't it? Would you like to see the flat?'

'Yes, please,' I said.

She wheezed her way upstairs with me creeping behind her and had to stop on the landing to draw breath. 'You go on, dear,' she said, gasping. 'I'm not as young as I used to be.'

The flat was incredibly overstuffed with ancient, inelegant furniture. Everything was patterned: walls, curtains, carpets, chairs, and the prevailing colours appeared to be brown, pink and mauve. But it was cheap. It was also smaller than I had expected.

I breathed in the scent of mothballs (the previous tenants could not have left very recently) and called down the stairs, 'You said three rooms in the advertisement.'

The answer came faintly back, muffled by the effort of renewed climbing and creaking wood: 'The kitchen's big enough to eat in.'

This was just about true. I should have to read more carefully if I went on searching. I looked out of the window at the sparse trees lining the road, the rows of shabby houses identical to the last television aerial, and thought what I was leaving behind.

The creaking ceased. I turned round and saw her leaning against a rather shaky bannister. 'My last tenants,' she said slowly, 'they ate in the kitchen all the time. But you couldn't have a baby here.'

I stared at her. I had told her on the front doorstep that I was pregnant.

'I mean, you haven't got the room,' she went on. 'And I'm a very light sleeper.'

'You didn't say no children in your advertisement,' I said, reverting to my newly acquired professional jargon.

'No ... well, it's not that. I mean, a two-year-old now ...' Her gaze wandered. 'But not a small baby.'

'I'm sorry,' I said. 'I'm wasting your time.'

'No,' she said, with a certain sharpness behind the vacancy, 'you could come for six months.'

'I'll tell my husband,' I said. I was getting quite smooth at this part. 'And I'll let you know.'

'She sounds insane,' said Malcolm.

'She probably is.' I was very tired. 'She's certainly odd. I think she just wants some money and some company without any inconvenience. Quite understandable, just awkward for us.'

'D'you want me to have a look at the flat?'

'No,' I said. 'If you can't picture it from my description, just be thankful.' I told him about the other one I had seen, a large basement flat with very little furniture and a landlord with lecherous eyes who murmured, 'Having a baby, are you?' smiled, raised an eyebrow and stripped me with a glance.

'Well, we're not going there,' said Malcolm at once. 'I'd never dare go to work. I think we should try agencies; we're getting all the nut cases by answering ads.'

When we were alone now we seemed to be always talking

about flats or worrying how to stretch the same few pounds in various directions. I was to find another job, anything, for a few months, to help out. We hardly ever made love now, and when we did it was rushed and somehow guilty, which it had never really been before. This dated from telling my mother I was pregnant.

'Flats are cheaper nearer town,' I said.

'I know.' He looked worried. 'But I'd have much further to travel to work.'

'You've got the car.'

'Yes. Val, I've been wondering. Maybe we ought to let the car go.'

'Don't be stupid.' I was outraged. 'We'd never get out; we'd have no fun at all. Maybe you can get a transfer.' It was a shock, knowing how much he loved the car.

We went to agencies and they wanted a fee for finding us a flat. We looked at flats together in the evenings. It was a pretty depressing business and we grew expert at translating the agents' reassuring words. 'Deep sink' meant chipped earthenware and no draining board. 'Gas fire' meant no electric point. 'Modernized' meant falling apart. We walked, talked and looked, and our time nearly ran out. About ten days before the wedding we found a tolerable flat of three rooms, kitchen and bathroom where children were permitted, upstairs in a semi-detached house (share garden) midway between town and home. It was, of course, more than we could really afford.

'I think we should settle for this,' Malcolm said.

'It's too expensive,' I said, although I knew he was right.

'Not really. Not when you think of the others.'

'Oh, it's good value,' I said. 'I just mean we can't afford it.'

'We can while you're working.' He looked apologetic.

'Yes,' I said. 'So what happens when I stop?'

Malcolm sat down. He looked tired. 'If we have to move, we'll move,' he said, 'but I think we should take it.' He still looked gorgeous but out of place, like an actor cast in the wrong sort of film.

'We don't have any fun these days,' I said sadly. I smiled at him to show there was no ill-feeling.

'I know,' he said. 'But we will.'

We took the flat. There was no time to look any further, anyway. The wedding was advancing upon us rapidly and irrevocably, like the express train in films my mother had described to me, and I was the heroine tied to the track. But there was no villain really. I had tied myself there.

Considering this period now, I suppose you could say I was resigned, except that the word suggests looking forward to a permanent state and I didn't envisage a lifetime like this. I don't think I allowed myself to look far ahead at all. The immediate decision was made and clear; there was no point in rehashing the same set of facts. I had caused myself enough agony. But I think that I planned in terms of a year; very vaguely, just along the lines of 'next year will be better'. I didn't consider the baby at all, except that next summer I would no longer have it inside me. With the wedding arranged I found, paradoxically, that for long stretches I could forget I was pregnant. Physically there was still little to remind me and what there was I determinedly ignored. When you have always been very active it is humiliating to have your body below par, and I planned to swim and play tennis as long as possible when the wedding rush was over.

We invited only the few people my mother could afford and even they were too many. I didn't want to see anyone. I went right off the idea of bridesmaids other than Jean, but I invited Sally and Marianne as guests. In the weeks before the wedding I alternated between shutting myself in the house (except when I was flat-hunting) and making defiant sorties into the village, where I looked everyone much too straight in the eye. There were a few embarrassing moments, but on the whole it passed off well.

It was a period of non-thinking, as if I had worn out my mind with worry beforehand and now it had quit, unbidden, for a rest. I glided like a puppet through all that had to be done and presented a cheerful yet serious exterior to my mother. But the worst was over. She had put everything into the talk we had had alone together. It was typical of her and it saved me. If she had been a person to open and re-open an issue I might have cracked.

The night before the wedding Malcolm and I went for a drive and made a half-hearted attempt at sex. But we were both too preoccupied.

'A fine time to go off it,' I said, to tease him. 'I shall divorce you.'

'Don't worry.' He was a shade too earnest. 'I'll be all the better tomorrow.'

And yet when we drove home and the moon was rising he looked so dark and dramatic, so fairy prince and film star, that I leaned across and surprised him with an almost savage kiss, while he was still parking the car. I wanted to cry; it was my first touch of feeling in weeks. He looked so wonderful and felt the same and smelt the same and kissed me back: what was I doing to him, to myself? The whole thing spun round me for a shattering second, as the room revolves when you are drunk.

And stopped, as it also does. The secret is not to close your eyes. You can get the same feeling of insane reality in an examination. (Did I voluntarily let myself in for this?) But you know it is worthwhile, or at least necessary. So the feeling passes. In my room that night I was calm as death. I could cope with Mother and Jean.

Our wedding took place very smoothly. The speeches were short and I wore a green suit.

PART 2

THIRTEEN

MALCOLM said in broadest Lancashire, 'Hullo, love. Ee, you do look lovely lying there.'

I opened my eyes. He hadn't talked like this since we – well, for a long time. 'Thank you very much,' I said. He was leaning on one elbow, looking at me. 'You look like something out of an X film,' I added.

'Aye, but it's legal now.'

'So are they, quite often. New gimmick. The right carrying-ons of the married couple.'

'Sort of " Carry On Fucking ",' said Malcolm. 'The last word in the Carry On series.' I giggled. 'Seriously though,' he said, dropping the accent, 'did you sleep well?'

I looked at him, innocently misunderstanding. 'Yes, fine,' I said.

'You know what I mean. Was I up to standard – for an old married man?'

'Not bad.'

'Well, you seemed to do all right.'

We had become suddenly self-conscious, faced with a Wedding Night. In the end we had got rather drunk and had one of our abandoned sessions, long overdue. It had been the only way. Now I felt very relaxed.

'It was rather terrific,' I said.

Malcolm smiled. 'You went to sleep very suddenly.'

'So I did. You must have worn me out.'

'Or you drank too much.'

'Charming. Probably both, actually.'

We lay in silence for a while, restfully. Then Malcolm said,

'Funny to think we can go to bed any time we like now. When was the last time we were actually in bed?'

I thought. 'April, I think. Before I started work. That afternoon when Mother was at the shop and Jean was at the pictures.'

'And we kept hoping Jean wouldn't change her mind and come home too soon.'

'That's right.'

'And we wondered if the neighbours would notice we were alone in the house.'

I laughed. 'Well, at least *that* doesn't matter any more.'

He ignored that. 'I make it only four times in bed altogether.'

I counted. Twice (briefly) at parties; one other time in another empty house. 'Yes, four,' I said.

'It's not much. We've got a lot to make up for. All those bushes and insects were a bit rough.'

'We didn't mind at the time.'

'No . . . it was worth it.'

'It was exciting.' I remembered, perversely, going for walks and wondering with a delicious sensation exactly when he would stop me and turn me round, which tree or pile of leaves would be the one. Dusk falling, tantalizingly slow, until at last we could risk cold fingers on skin. Fun, sometimes, to be passive and wait, making no approach. Fun also to pretend reluctance and resist, fight him off, not so much as to be discouraging but enough to put extra zest into the proceedings, like a shot of whisky in tea.

'It was uncomfortable though.'

'You appeared to enjoy it at the time.'

'Sure I did. I still got bitten to death.'

'So did I. Worse, if anything. I wasn't wearing trousers.'

'Just as well, or we wouldn't have got very far.'

'We got too far. I *should*'ve worn trousers.'

'Oh, shut up,' said Malcolm with unexpected force. 'We've been into all that. Aren't we having fun again?'

'Yes.'

64

'Well, then.' He reached for a cigarette. 'What's the time?'

I looked at my watch, which I only removed in the bath. During the summer there was always a wide, pale strap-mark on my wrist. 'Twenty past eleven.'

'Not bad. I bet we're both lying here kidding ourselves one of our mothers is going to appear with tea and start cooking breakfast.'

'If that's a hint,' I said, 'you can carry on hinting, too. If the bridegroom can't wait on the bride after violently ravishing her, it's a poor look-out for the younger generation.'

'Oh, all right,' said Malcolm, with exaggerated reluctance. 'Just let me finish this cigarette.' He paused, then said abruptly, 'Did you enjoy it yesterday?'

'The wedding?'

'Yes.'

'Mm.'

'You looked great.'

'Thanks. I tried.'

'I thought your mother was going to cry, but she didn't.'

'No, she didn't. Yours did. God knows why.'

'Only heart-broken at losing the best son a mother ever had. No, seriously, she always cries at weddings. She did at my cousin Connie's wedding and she can't stand her.'

'There you are.'

'Oh, come in, Val. I know you're not crazy about each other, but it's not as bad as that.'

'No. I'm just being bitchy.' I had, in fact, enjoyed the tears of Malcolm's mother coursing through her powder as she stood in her so carefully chosen navy suit that she called a costume, with white shoes and gloves and plastic handbag and a pink straw hat with an artificial rose on her head. My own mother had looked so unquestionably right in a grey-blue dress and coat, with black everything, meriting a glance of appreciation not the shocked attention of mesmerized eye-balls. If Malcolm's mother had ever had children at boarding school she'd have embarrassed them so much at public functions they'd have hanged themselves at the earliest subsequent opportunity. I smiled.

'You are rather bitchy sometimes,' Malcolm said.

'I know. I just admitted it. Does it bother you?'

'I'm not sure. I don't think you ought to be but I rather like it. It's sort of ... feminine.'

'But I'm not very feminine,' I said. Someone had told me this recently; I had forgotten who it was.

'Aren't you?' He reached out a hand.

'Oh *yes*,' I said crossly, 'but I mean – oh well.' I gave up suddenly.

'Is that nice?'

'Mm.'

'Is it?'

'You know it is.'

'D'you mind not having a honeymoon?'

'No.'

'We can have one right here, can't we?'

'Yes. Oh yes.'

'Well.' He sighed. 'I suppose I must go and get the breakfast.'

'Malcolm –'

'What?'

'Don't stop. Please.'

'What?'

'Please go on.'

'You mean like this?'

'Yes. Yes. Oh God.'

He moved closer. 'It was dark last night. Now I can watch you.'

Some time later when I had stopped shuddering I said, 'You wait. I'll get my own back. I'll punish you.'

'Good,' said Malcolm, triumphant. 'I was hoping you would.'

So you see we started well.

FOURTEEN

I got a job in a library, a temporary one while someone they valued who had promised to return was away having a baby. Oh, full of irony. I liked working odd hours so that some days I could sleep all morning. Malcolm wasn't too keen when I pushed him out of bed at eight or when he had to fetch me from the library twelve hours later. He didn't like me working Saturdays either and having time off mid-week. But the nine-till-five days suited him.

It was a good job for me. When we were slack I could read quite a lot provided I managed to look as if I was doing something else, and even when we were busy I picked up the routine fairly fast and it was fun to see what books people were taking out. But, more than any of this, I felt a positively sensual satisfaction in being surrounded by books. The rows of them all round the walls, all lined up together in their jackets, all delicious and different and full of words gave me a shiver of delight. I felt peaceful, warm and reassured. It occurred to me how comparatively little I had appreciated the school library while I was there, the wonderful quiet and richness of it. I had associated it too much with working for exams. It had been too functional, too stripped of pleasure, of reading for reading's sake. Now I felt a great resurgence of energy. I brought piles of books back to the flat.

'Leave some for the customers,' said Malcolm. He seemed surprised.

'I read quickly,' I said. 'This way I can read heaps of new stuff before it goes out. If I wait till everyone's finished with them I'll be a customer myself again.'

'You like the job, don't you?' He spoke gently.

'Well, it's certainly better than the shop.'

I made friends with Sandra, who had bright blonde hair and an infinitesimal solitaire, and she told me the senior librarian or whatever she was called was 'a poppet'. She looked like a dried prune, but it turned out Sandra was right. She was a poppet. She was incredibly kind to me, as a beginner, and infinitely tolerant of Sandra, who tended to rush off so promptly as to be almost early to meet her fiancé, whom she called her boy-friend. Miss Mills often talked in clichés but somehow managed to do it lovably. 'You're only young once,' she'd say, watching Sandra's golden head and curving body perilously balanced on four-inch heels as she ran flat out towards Johnny's motor-bike. Her dress was so tight that I stared with disbelief as she climbed on the back of the bike and the skirt shot way up to her thighs without rending. 'He's a nice boy,' said Miss Mills as they roared off into the evening. 'She's known him three years and they're saving hard.' She sighed. 'It's so difficult for young people these days.' She sounded really sympathetic; there was no trace of envy in her voice. 'No wonder you want to work as long as you can. Take our Mrs Carey now. Her husband's studying to get a degree and she's coming back here as soon as she can. Her sister's going to look after the baby. I'm sure it will work out very well.' And yet to look at Miss Mills would have made you expect a tirade against the evils of the working mother.

It was Sandra who made me feel old, though. She was eighteen but in a sense she was enjoying youth I had never had. I didn't exactly envy her – at least I would not have changed persons with her – but I recognized a light-heartedness I had never really felt. My first set of public exams were her first and her last; at sixteen she had left school and earned money and courted Johnny. She had got, within her chosen limits, all she wanted. I had cast my net far wider; but it had broken. I felt the sense of alienation even musically: Sally was totally for pop and awe-inspiringly knowledgeable about it. Not that I hadn't collected through my teens and enjoyed the top twenty and the pop shows on TV, but, influenced by my mother perhaps, I had played Beethoven and Mozart as well, and Malcolm and I had always been a couple of squares with Sinatra and Ella and Brubeck. I had gone to plenty of dances, but they were not the highlight of my week. I had never had much money to spend on clothes and make-up, so had chosen what suited me and was cheap to maintain, like below-chin-length straight hair (a simple matter for me of cutting and growth) and more eye-liner than lipstick. My mother and I got clothes a bit cheaper from the shop and they lasted a long time. We looked after them instinctively so that they never got badly marked the way other people's did. We pressed them often and washed or cleaned when necessary. We had to be very sure when we bought something that we really liked it, as it was going to be around us for years. Our hem-lines were always on the move. Luckily we were the same size so that, although each of us had a small basic wardrobe, this was in practice virtually doubled. It could have been trebled as Jean grew older, but tragically she began shooting up.

Sandra and her mother could have none of this as her mother was fat. She called it plump. Sandra would probably go the same way, but as of now her waist was tiny. Thinking of my own and the fate that was creeping up on it, I was extra conscious of Sandra's slenderness. 'Besides, I wouldn't be seen dead in my mum's things,' said Sandra, outraged. 'Your mum must've been ever so modern if you could wear her stuff.' She giggled. 'You should just see my mum when she's all dressed up. Like the dog's dinner.' I gathered from other conversations that this implied no disrespect : to Sandra it was simply a fact. Similarly her mother was twenty-five years older than she was, and had to wear glasses. I had not thought whether my mother was modern: our tastes were alike. We would choose the same colours, the same shapes. Whether a sweater was worn inside or outside a skirt, a dress with or without its belt were the only matters that might divide us.

Sandra brought sandwiches for lunch because she was saving up. Her mother provided them for her out of the two pounds a week Sandra gave her, some of which she generally had to return at the end of the week when Sandra was broke. She became broke very effectively by dividing what was left, after paying her mother, into two halves. One was immediately placed in the post office, where it was firmly fixed as if cemented, the other became Sandra's pocket (clothes, records, hair, make-up, stockings) money for the week. She lived within running distance of the library. She didn't smoke – at least she didn't buy cigarettes but always accepted mine or her mother's or Miss Mills' with a 'Oh, I shouldn't really,' followed (too rapidly for escape) by 'But I will.' All the time I was there Miss Mills never hardened herself to combat this, but I very soon started lighting up for myself, smiling at Sandra and telling her how wise she was not to smoke.

Sandra said she was looking forward to getting married because then she would be two pounds a week better off. I could not think what was holding her back; if she'd been packing the post office with her current determination for the whole three years she'd known Johnny, she'd very soon have more in there than anyone was allowed. I teased her about this and then it came out; they were waiting till Johnny was twenty-one so that they could get a mortgage. 'Johnny says we must start off properly.'

It did seem ironic; it did make me reel and question myself. Was this what I was saving Jean from? And yet it was impossible to dislike Sandra. She was nearly always cheerful, very good with the customers and with a fantastic memory for faces; genuinely kind ('Don't you feel well? Go on, have a lie-down, I'll manage') and about certain sections of the library surprisingly well-informed. There seemed to be considerable division of labour : Sandra knew the location and contents of every crime and romantic novel in the place, Miss Mills was a walking non-fiction catalogue, and Mrs Carey, whom I was replacing, was the classical and modern novel expert. No, it wasn't policy; it had just happened. 'Aren't we lucky?' said Miss Mills. It was clear she considered herself the fortunate leader of a perfect team. I became so conditioned to Sandra that I began to regard her as superhuman until I one day discovered her huddled in the washroom after being sick, her eyes shiny with tears.

'Whatever's the matter?'

'It's my stomach,' she replied vaguely, 'and I haven't got nothing with me.' Her mascara had run and her face was crumpled with pain : she looked not a day over twelve.

'All right, I'll get you something,' I said.

'Will you?' She sighed with relief and told me what to get. 'I couldn't ask Miss Mills, not at her age.'

This delicate scruple was rather beyond me, but I went out and came back and gave Sandra her parcel, pushed some tablets into her mouth and banished her to the lavatory. She came back much later, still very white, but calmer.

'Better?' I inquired.

'A bit.' She leaned on the desk.

'Coffee's coming up shortly.' It was the first time I had got to it; she always made it for both of us.

'Thanks ever so much.' Her face contorted as another cramp seized her. You could see her relaxing, inch by inch, as it eased off. 'D'you ever get it as bad as this?'

'No,' I said, 'I never did.' She stared at me. 'I'm pregnant,' I said.

'Oh.' Her surprise was obvious. Clearly Miss Mills had not mentioned it. 'Oh, are you? Fancy you not saying. Congratulations.'

'Thank you,' I said.

And yet in spite of aching breasts and occasional nausea

and a maddening dependence on the lavatory – oh, all the repulsive stuff you are so cheerfully warned about as if it doesn't matter a damn – every time I told a new person I still felt I was telling a lie.

FIFTEEN

'I didn't know you could cook,' Malcolm said.

'Cook?'

He pointed at the stew we had nearly finished.

'If you call this cooking,' I said, 'then anyone can cook.'

'Go on, tell me.'

'Tell you what?'

'How you made it.'

'Why? Are *you* going to make it?'

'No. I just want to hear you.'

'Oh, good Lord.' I heard the Lydia Bennet in me escaping and curbed it. 'Well, it couldn't be simpler. You just buy everything and chop it up and throw it in with Oxo and water and cook it for four or five hours in the oven.'

He finished eating and ran some bread round his plate to soak up the gravy. It looked awful, but I supposed it was a compliment. 'Go on,' he said, 'what else can you cook?'

'Are you still hungry?'

'Course I'm not. But can you cook other things? I mean, why haven't we had this before?'

'You mean why have we had so much egg and chips and spaghetti on toast and soup?'

He grinned. 'Yeah.'

'Because they're cheaper, quicker and easier, that's why. This is a long job. Week-ends only, for a start.'

'It's worth it.'

'Your mother cooked things like this. It's just the same.' I was being mischievous.

'No, she put kidneys in. I don't go for kidneys. Can you do pies as well? And cakes?'

I sighed. 'Oh God, Malcolm, you're making me feel sick. Yes, I can, sort of. Pastry better than cakes. My mother and I got hooked on those mixes. She'd get in at five and we could be eating the cake by seven.'

'Did she teach you to cook?'

'No. She said I had enough to do.' I paused, then hurried on. 'She took the view I could pick it up when I needed it. She was right. You just buy a book and do what it says. Then later on, I suppose, you can make up things for yourself.'

Malcolm sat back comfortably and lit a cigarette. 'Must be a secret gift girls have. One of your more respectable gifts.'

'Nonsense.' I was annoyed. 'My father taught my mother to cook.'

'Did he?'

'Well? What's wrong with that?'

'Nothing. I was just surprised. Don't be so touchy, Val. You know Dad can't cook and I don't think Mum ever wanted him to. I'm just ... not used to the idea.'

'It's not cissy,' I said, 'if that's what you mean.'

'No, of course it's not. I mean there are chefs and that ... Val, what is this?'

'What?'

'I mean, here we are practically having a row because your father could cook and mine can't. I mean, what does it matter?'

'It doesn't,' I said, 'but you might remember to offer me a cigarette now and then.'

'Oh, I'm sorry.' He took them out. 'Was that what you were mad about?'

'I don't want one now,' I said. 'It's just the principle. You're taking me for granted.'

'Not really.' He got up and came to stand behind my chair, stroking the back of my neck. He said in Cockney, 'You'd still be a smashing bird if you couldn't boil water.'

SIXTEEN

ONE day in the morning before my one-till-eight shift I wrote a letter. It took me a long time.

Dear Mrs Franklin,

I don't know whether you have heard but I got married recently. I am expecting a baby early in April. It's not easy to write and tell you all this.

I really want to ask you a favour. I am working in a library for three or four months, so I have access to a lot of books and time for some reading; when I leave I shall have time to do more. I don't want to backslide and lose everything we worked so hard for. I am forgetting my Latin already. Do you think if I read some of the books you recommended and the ones on the London suggested reading list, I could do some essays for you? I know you have all your school marking to do but I would be enormously grateful if you could possibly keep me going like this.

I hope you had a good holiday this summer.

Yours sincerely,

Valerie (Ayden) Ross

The idea had been germinating secretly for some time. After all, no trained athlete in his senses would allow his body to get weak and overweight for lack of exercise. Lazing around in the holidays was one thing, but deliberately allowing your mind to rot for an unspecified period after all the years it had taken to make it reach even this level ... I knew I was asking a lot; in my last year at school I had begun to realize something of the work Mrs Franklin had to do. But

I had confidence in her; I could not believe she would let me down. There was certainly no one else I could ask.

I had brought all my books with me, naturally, but there was small accommodation for them at the flat. Our solitary bookshelf wobbled unsteadily and appeared suited rather to the display of porcelain egg-cups. Anything as heavy as a book seemed to give it the jitters. I packed in what I could, a lot of the paper-backs, anyway, and piled the rest on the floor of the bedroom and living-room. They looked solid and re-assuring. When Malcolm's mother came she asked if I didn't find they collected a lot of dust. Malcolm himself was surprised to see how many books I had, and I discovered that he was in the habit of buying science fiction or thriller paper-backs and throwing them away. There's a lot you don't know about each other after only a year.

I didn't feel married. It was as though we were living in sin with everyone's permission. A strange feeling. My mother and Jean came to see us and we chatted casually about every-day things. Malcolm's parents came for the occasional meal and once Malcolm's father said (in his wife's absence), 'So she can cook as well.' He winked at Malcolm. It was a very crude wink. 'My word, if I were your age.' At this point Mrs Ross returned and he cleared his throat and said hastily, 'I was just telling Valerie, love, what a good meal that was.' Even so, his fatherly hug on the doorstep was a trifle too long and he managed to bump into parts of me he could well have avoided. It confirmed an odd feeling I had had since before the wedding. The news of my pregnancy seemed to have made Mr Ross's behaviour vaguely suggestive, whereas before he had treated me remotely, with respect, even awe. I didn't quite realize how angry I was until I said to Malcolm, 'Your father's a lecherous old bastard' after they had gone, and heard my voice shake.

'He's only jealous,' said Malcolm easily. 'I don't suppose Mum's very sexy.'

'That's hardly the point,' I said. 'I'm not a Mum-substitute.'

'Why? What happened?' He seemed puzzled.

'Well, that remark at dinner, when your mother was out of the room.'

'Oh Val, that wasn't anything.' He took refuge behind a newspaper.

'All boys together, was it? Well, I didn't like it, nor the way he kisses me good night, *nor* the way he looks at me. It's all a sight too familiar.'

Malcolm lowered the paper. 'I don't think he means any harm by it. It's a sort of compliment in a way. He admires you and he envies me. He used to be quite a lad, you know, and now he's a bit past it.'

'Then someone should tell him,' I said. 'And maybe I'm just the right person.'

'Oh Val.' Malcolm looked uneasy. 'Don't let's have any trouble.'

'All right, you stop him. Or I will. I don't like being regarded as a hot bit of stuff or whatever it's called, by your father of all people.'

The quarrel pervaded the rest of the evening, but as usual we made it up in bed. In the morning I had almost forgotten about it. The next day was Sunday and we piled food in the car and drove into the country. There were places quiet enough to eat in but not quiet enough for anything else and we laughed at ourselves because the warm autumn sun made us feel sexy and there was nothing we could do about it. We didn't like to return to our own more familiar and less crowded woods.

We forgot the idea gradually and drove back by a roundabout route to avoid the traffic, and listened to music on the radio. We stopped at a pub to buy beer and in the evening Jeff came round with his current girl-friend Marie and it was all quite fun. We'd had a whole day without a cross word.

Malcolm did surprise things, too, like arriving home and saying, 'Come on, get your coat; we're going out', because (as I only discovered when we reached the theatre) he had got tickets for a jazz concert. It was really good and gave you the sort of glow no other single thing can, a curious exhilaration as if compounded of drink and sex and mountain air. I drove, going back, and the feel of the car was the final touch of bliss. Probably people who don't think much are really happier, though I've never envied them. But I was pure sensation that night.

SEVENTEEN

MALCOLM said, 'It's beginning to show.' He was lying in bed, watching me undress.

I pulled the nightdress quickly over my head and let it fall. 'Yes, isn't it?'

'It suits you, though,' he added.

Our bedroom in the flat had a wash-basin, so I turned my back on him to clean my teeth. I made teeth-cleaning sounds instead of answering.

'Val.'

'Mm.'

'We haven't talked about it at all. Since we got married, I mean.'

I spat in the basin.

He went on, just a little awkwardly, 'You go off to the clinic but you never tell me what it's like. Shouldn't you be doing exercises or something?'

I started to gargle. I could not imagine what he wanted to hear about a place where I joined all the other cow-like women for routine examinations and tried to remain detached.

'We haven't even thought of names.'

I spat, finally, and put down the glass. 'There's plenty of time.' I still did not want to turn round and face him, so I started brushing my hair. I wondered if it would really benefit from the blue-black rinse Sally always recommended when I let her cut it.

'Aren't you interested?'

I turned round. 'Not very.'

We looked at each other for what seemed a long time.

He said, 'I thought you'd feel better about it after we got married.'

I said, 'Why? Do you?'

'Yes.'

'Well, good for you.' I started moving about the room, too agitated to go to bed.

'Oh, don't be like that.' He seemed distressed. 'We've been getting on so well. Haven't we?'

'Yes. Sure.'

'It's just that we've never talked about the baby.'

I wondered if it was worth trying to explain the refuge I had found in ignoring the whole situation during the past weeks. I had never before so fully appreciated the meaning of burying one's head in the sand. With me working, we had not really worried about money; we had been able to enjoy ourselves again having faced everyone and done everything necessary. The flat was pleasant, I enjoyed my job, I looked forward intensely to studying again. My body was tough and with determination I could very largely ignore any physical discomfort.

Why could he not do the same? Why could he not see that films and music, dancing and driving, looking the way he did (even now in bed in green pyjamas) were all exciting and all part of our relationship as I remembered it at its best, and that the worried parental stuff was horribly incongruous and repulsive?

I said, following my own train of thought, 'I don't want to see you like that.'

He looked puzzled. Puzzled yet very attractive. It was annoying in the extreme. 'Like what?'

'Oh – ' I exploded a deep breath and a lot of surprising vehemence – 'like a bloody expectant father.'

He almost laughed, although he looked shocked. It was a strange combination: more the look you get on a girl's face when she has been told a blue joke and is uncertain how to react. He said simply, 'But I am.' I didn't answer, and he went on, 'You *are* having a baby and it *is* my baby and I *am* interested. What's wrong with that?'

'It doesn't suit you,' I said.

His eyes narrowed and he suddenly looked very dark and threatening. That was better. 'Wouldn't it suit me a lot less,' he said, 'if I didn't give a damn about you or the baby?'

I shrugged my shoulders.

'Look,' he said. 'Let's face facts. You *are* pregnant and we *are* married. That's all. So why can't we discuss it?'

'There's nothing to discuss. You said it all.'

He sighed with exasperation. There was a slight pause, and when he spoke again his tone had changed. 'You're not scared, are you?' he said.

'Scared? Of what?'

'Of having the baby of course.' He looked rather pleased with himself, as if he had just hit on a clever solution to a problem. I could see him preparing to be sympathetic.

'No.'

He went on regardless. 'There's nothing to be ashamed of if you are. I'm sure everyone is. But it can't be too bad if so many people get through it. You can read books about it so you know what to expect and they do have all those drugs to stop it hurting.'

'I said no.'

He looked at me searchingly. 'You would tell me if you were scared?'

'Oh, for God's sake, yes.'

'All right.' He lay down. 'I'm sorry, I'm pushing you. Come to bed.'

I waited a bit, wanting to make a gesture of rejection, but it was getting cold and I felt a fool trailing round in my nightdress. I got in and lay down, apart from him. He put the light out.

'Val.' His voice was different in the dark: stronger, softer, I don't know. 'Friends again?'

'Sure.'

His hand reached out gently and touched my breasts.

'Don't,' I said. 'They're sore,' although normally I let him touch them, sore or not.

'Sorry.' His hand moved lower down. 'Are you sore there?'

I didn't answer. I wanted to move violently away but I seemed transfixed and the fact that we had just quarrelled only made it more exciting.

'Or there?'

I moved in spite of myself.

'Oh Val. Darling.' He pulled me into his arms and started kissing me. He didn't say darling very often. I found myself responding just as if there were nothing wrong at all. Soon I couldn't think, only move and feel.

'We're all right, aren't we?' he said. I couldn't answer; I was swept along irresistibly. Pull one lever and all the machinery glides into motion and to your own surprise you can't stop it. But right through to the end, through the chaos and heat of his pleasure and mine, I was conscious of his body as though it was a steel strap.

EIGHTEEN

MRS Franklin's answer came a week later.

Dear Valerie,

Thank you for your letter. I had in fact heard your news but I very much appreciated your taking the trouble to write to me yourself. I realize you must have found it difficult.

Of course I shall be glad to help you all I can although my free time is, as you know, extremely limited. I am enclosing a suggested reading list and some essay subjects based on it, but there is no need for you to feel bound to limit yourself to this. You know as well as I do by now what is worth reading. I'm glad you are working in a library as I'm sure you will find this far more congenial than the shop.

My husband and I had a very enjoyable holiday in France in August, but it seems a long time ago now since beginning the new term and plunging into auditions for the play. We are now in the midst of rehearsals – my only excuse for my delay in answering your letter.

With very best wishes

Yours sincerely,

Claire Franklin

I sat and just looked at the letter after I had read it, aware of all it did not say. I knew I was being unreasonable. She had agreed to help me; her letter was perfectly pleasant and friendly. What did I want? Lies about it not mattering, not being a waste, a disappointment? Or was it more than that? Already there seemed a chill of remoteness in the letter as if I was not vividly in her mind as she wrote. Surely I could not be forgotten so soon, passed off the assembly line, finished;

I knew that literally, of course, she remembered me, but something of the closeness we had enjoyed while working together had gone. There were other classes, other candidates, more real to her already. It was natural; in the ordinary way it would not have mattered at all.

I started working. There was so much I had not read; my task was enormous. I began with *Paradise Lost* of which I knew only the first two books. It was difficult to feel affection for Milton, but admiration came easily. It brought back school very clearly, too : early lessons on epic similes. I read aloud to myself and got drunk chanting the words. It was much easier than it had been before, reading silently at sixteen opposite Jean at the table with all the dedication demanded by exams, pushing myself endlessly through books one and two and memorizing the arguments of each fallen angel. Not a poet to be read late at night when you were tired from a day's school : top concentration was needed not to lose grip on the lengthy, rolling sentences. At first I had been resentful but now I could see the majesty of it and it seemed the only possible style for such a theme.

Appreciation was one thing, analysis another. I read and made notes. Malcolm in his chair was busy identifying with James Bond. There was a beautiful silence and I seemed sure of a good evening's work. But after about an hour he got up and I heard the click of the television set as he switched it on.

'Mustn't miss the fight,' he said.

I looked up, still half with Milton.

'Boxing,' he explained.

It became impossible very quickly, so after a while I picked up my things and moved to the bedroom. He followed me.

'What are you doing?'

'Reading.'

'Can't you read in there?'

'I can't concentrate.'

He looked surprised. 'You used to.'

'Not on Milton.'

'Oh. D'you have to read Milton?'

'I want to. Does it matter?'

'Well, if you have to do it in here . . .'

'You've got the television.' I turned back to the book.

He went out. I was distantly aware of a click and he called out, 'I've turned it off.'

I was annoyed. I didn't want him to martyr himself and I was comfortably settled in the bedroom. I called back, 'Don't be silly, Malcolm. This way we can both please ourselves.' I pushed the door to. There was complete silence for a few minutes, then softly, a noise not words, the rhythm of the boxing commentary began again. I slid back into Eden.

NINETEEN

THE next month was very productive. It was no longer possible to forget that I was pregnant, but physically I felt better than I had done for some time. It seemed as if studying was a form of compensation. I finished my Milton project, although I knew it was a large draught. I read books about Milton, agreeing and disagreeing violently (sometimes muttering 'That's what I thought' or alternatively 'Rubbish') as I read. After finishing *Paradise Lost* I assessed Milton's attempt to justify the words of God to man; then I went on to *Paradise Regained* and wrote an essay explaining why I found it unsatisfactory. I read *Samson Agonistes* and produced pages on the influence of Greek tragedy. Finally I posted my three essays to Mrs Franklin. However bad they might be, I had a sense of accomplishment.

Jean continued to call in most Sundays, however briefly. I was never able to ask her if she had been teased at school, though it was painfully easy to imagine how bravely she would stick up for me. Malcolm was very good with her and it was obvious that her crush on him had, if anything, increased. She loved the flat because it was ours. To her there was enormous glamour in being married and having somewhere to live. I felt, as I had felt for some time, that we were merely playing a game.

Malcolm helped the man downstairs with the garden. We hardly ever saw him or his wife as they were both out at work and so were we. But my days were numbered whereas hers would continue. She was not pregnant and for that, without speaking to her, I disliked her intensely. I caught myself glaring at her waistline. She made matters worse by wearing tight, wide belts.

I was first aware of how time was running out (like the sand in the hourglass, a childhood nightmare after seeing *The Wizard of Oz*) when I reached the library one day and found Miss Mills waving a tiny card which bore a fanciful portrait of a stork. 'She's had a little boy,' she exclaimed. 'Isn't it wonderful?'

'Oh good,' I said. I forgot Miss Mills's sterling qualities; for an instant she joined the hordes of people I had spent my life despising, for no good reason, doubtless, but that did not weaken the feeling: people I met in the street with my mother, people who wore no make-up, said things twice, called babies 'little mites' and 'scraps' as if there was some merit in their smallness, cooed over animals and children indiscriminately, peppered everything with 'Well, I never' or 'That's what I always say', and (when I was particularly silent) leaned forward to inquire, 'What's the matter, Valerie? Cat got your tongue? My word, we *are* a solemn little girl this morning.' As I grew older I learned to save myself with words, but the secret longing to machine-gun them into pulp remained. Sometimes it worried me: I was like Hitler and God would punish me. But I had only to meet them again to feel justified.

'A lovely little boy,' Miss Mills went on, though she could not possibly have seen it. 'Seven pounds six ounces. Born the day before yesterday. Isn't that splendid?'

It made you wonder whatever she had expected. Surely it was all as near normal as you could get. 'Marvellous,' I said. 'Do excuse me; I don't feel very well.' I almost ran into the washroom and locked myself in the lavatory. It reminded me now of school where it had been the only place where you could cry in peace.

What a fool I was; I was being absurd. But the repulsiveness of my situation overcame me. Here I was doing something that everyone around me regarded as delightful but which just made me sick – in every sense of the word. The prospect ahead of me was messy, painful and revolting. The end product was something I (to put it very mildly indeed) simply did not want. Sensible Marianne, or sensible David. I too should have taken tablets. I should have jumped off tables and swallowed gin. I should even – well, I should have done something, instead of wandering round in a panic, confiding in people and letting Malcolm marry me. Where the hell did I think it was all going to lead? It was hard enough now finding time to read when I worked all day and Malcolm wanted my company in the evening. How much worse would it be when I had a screaming baby to attend to? Mrs Carey's time had come and gone; mine was approaching. There was no way out now. But there had to be. I couldn't be trapped. I had always been able to save myself: I had been so strong and certain. I put my head between my knees as far as was possible nowadays, and the tiny room revolved with a drunken lurch. My face was damp and hot.

There was a shuffling noise outside as of hesitant feet. A knock. Then a voice. Miss Mills was asking, 'Are you all right, Valerie?'

'Yes,' I said. 'I'm all right.'

TWENTY

MARIANNE looked different : radiant, sleek, well-groomed. I thought she must be engaged at least; I had not seen her since September. But it turned out she was just happy because David was being nice to her. She sat on my sofa and pulsated with joy. If I had not been fond of her it would have been embarrassing.

'He comes round three or four nights a week,' she said and paused. She seemed to expect amazement on my part that she could be the lucky recipient of such a favour.

'Well, why shouldn't he?' I demanded. 'He's got a gorgeous girl-friend.'

She blushed; it was odd that I could still embarrass her. 'Oh,' she said, 'he has a lot to do.'

It was annoying to see him receiving such kudos for behaving, at last, like a normal human being. But I was pleased to see Marianne and didn't want to offend her. She obviously wanted to talk about David's wonderful goodness, so I made coffee and let her talk. He was actually phoning on the nights he'd promised to phone, it seemed. (And to think some people no longer believed in miracles.)

'But how are you, Val?' Marianne suddenly cut through her monologue. 'You're looking very well.'

I laughed. It was the kindest reaction I could find. 'Oh Marianne, who are you kidding? Let's face it, I look awful. You don't have to be polite, honestly.'

'You don't look awful to me. I think it suits you.'

I sat down opposite her. 'Well,' I said, 'that's not how I feel. In fact I can't think of anything that suits me less.'

Marianne was never slow in conversation, though on paper she had always displayed most uncharacteristic lack of perception. 'Oh Val,' she said, and all her gaiety vanished. 'Isn't it any better?'

I lit a cigarette. 'I think it's worse, suddenly. For a while I forgot about it somehow, but it got me, quite recently: I hate babies. I don't want it. I – I'd like to have it this minute and drown it, I think.'

Marianne was shaking her head. 'Oh no, you don't mean that.'

'I damn well do. I don't want it, Marianne. I don't know what to do with it. It's beginning to be real; well, look at me, it's not surprising, is it? And I don't want it.'

Marianne squeezed my hand. 'Don't say that,' she said gently. 'I think you're so lucky. I've been thinking about you for months and wishing I could – only David would never forgive me, so I can't, of course.'

I stared at her. 'You want a baby? You actually want one?'

She nodded. She said simply, 'I love David so much. If I could only have his baby I – I'd be over the moon.'

'Pity you can't have this one and pretend.'

'Oh dear.' Marianne looked guilty. 'I'm sorry.'

'No.' I made an effort. 'I'm being a swine. Of course you feel the way you do. You're in love with David.'

Marianne hesitated. She said, 'Aren't you – isn't it any better? I thought maybe . . .'

'No,' I said. She didn't look at me. 'We get on fine in bed,' I went on, trying to be fair. 'Works like a charm, as ever. But that's all.'

Marianne raised her head. 'Funny, isn't it?' she said. 'I'm so crazy about David and I still don't . . . you know. Hardly at all.' She looked worried. 'D'you think there's something wrong with me?'

'No.' It was obvious to me that neither of us had got the right man, but I could not say this. 'I'm sure a lot of people are the same.'

'David would be awfully upset if he knew,' Marianne said in a low voice as if he might be listening at the door.

'He doesn't know?'

'No, of *course* not.' She looked shocked at the very suggestion. 'He'd feel awful.'

'Maybe he could do something to help.'

'No. I was always the same, with everyone.' She seemed resigned again.

'So – what happens? You just pretend all the time?'

She nodded.

'But how can you? I never could if I didn't make it.'

She shook her head, smiling. 'It's easy. And it makes David so happy. I – I even told him I'd never felt it before. I said I didn't feel anything with the others.' She looked at me defensively, although I had not spoken. 'Well, it's not really a lie. I never loved anyone else.'

'That's true enough. I'll be your witness if you need one. So – is that why he doesn't mind about the others?' I had often wanted to ask her this, but without an introduction it seemed such a rude question.

'Well,' said Marianne guardedly, 'I said there were only two anyway.'

I took a deep breath. 'Oh,' I said. I thought it over. 'Why two?' I asked eventually. 'Why not just one?'

'I thought he'd be less jealous of two,' said Marianne. 'One sounds sort of special.'

'I suppose so.' Really she was very clever. 'Are you sure there's no risk of his finding out?'

'Oh Val, don't.' She shivered instantly. 'I suppose there must be really, a bit anyway, but it's been all right so far.'

She looked so scared that I had to reassure her. 'Oh, he won't find out,' I said. 'And anyway, after all this time he'd just have to understand. Don't look so worried.'

Marianne was fidgeting, watching her hands as she moved them. 'I wish he'd been the first,' she said, 'honest I do.'

It seemed very pathetic. I wanted to put my arms round

her and tell her it didn't matter and he was lucky to have her anyway, first or last.

'First thoughts are not always best,' I said, 'as we've both discovered.'

She looked up. 'D'you know,' she said gently, 'I never thought you would. With Malcolm I mean. I thought you'd got it all worked out, not like me.'

'Yes,' I said, 'so did I.'

'I thought you were getting the best of both worlds.' She smiled.

'So I was.' I lay back in the chair and shut my eyes. 'Remember how we kept going just a little bit further each time and thinking it was all right so long as we didn't go any further next time?'

'Yes.'

'And so on. I never thought I'd take any chances with Malcolm; it just crept up on me. Quite ridiculous. Unnecessary. God knows why we didn't get caught the first time; we were really careless.' It still shook me to remember it. After that it had been hard to refuse with Malcolm saying, 'You did before; why not again? Come on, Val,' and being persuasive and knowing I wanted to anyway. Unfair to blame him, though. I could have refused.

I opened my eyes and my shape met me. Reminiscing, I had briefly forgotten it.

'And here I am,' I said bitterly. 'Just look at me.'

'It's not bad really.'

'Yes, but going on till April? It's ridiculous. I shall burst like a frog. Oh God, Marianne, can you imagine what it will be like by April?'

'It'll be nearly over.' She was somehow almost pleading with me. 'Can't you look at it that way? I'll come over and sit with it so you can go out.'

'You *are* sweet,' I said. It was the nearest I could get to hugging her. 'I hope you marry David and have lots of kids if that's what you want.'

She shook her head. 'No. I mustn't be greedy.'

'Oh Marianne, don't give me that stuff about not being good enough. Why ever shouldn't you marry David?'

'It just won't happen.' She was obstinate as usual. 'So I'm not going to hope. It's silly to hope for things you know won't happen.'

'I suppose so,' I said. 'If you're really sure they won't.'

TWENTY-ONE

THE rest of November passed in a hail of well-meaning and good advice. My mother made maternity clothes for me and this – knowing she hated the sewing-machine even more than I did – touched me deeply. She said I looked depressed and I said I was tired. She wanted to know if I was eating and resting sensibly and how much longer I was going to work.

Malcolm, too, was interested in this. He had suddenly remembered that we hadn't saved very much and soon there would be nothing coming in to save.

'Look,' he said firmly, 'we'll just have to put away more each week. We've got to buy all the stuff for the baby.' He looked at me warily, no longer sure how I would react to the fatal word.

'I thought the adoring grandparents were supposed to do all that,' I said.

'Well, they can't buy everything.'

'Why not? They're a lot more interested in this baby than I am. If they want it to have things, they can buy them. What does it need anyway? A pram and some nappies. They can surely buy that much.'

'Oh Val, it's got to have clothes and a cot and loads of things.'

'Why? Why can't it sleep in its pram in a blanket? It doesn't need clothes; it's not going anywhere.'

He looked amused yet concerned. 'Oh, you know what I mean.'

'The hell with it,' I said. 'Why don't I just give you my

pay each week from now till Christmas and you can buy it whatever you like?'

'That's not what I meant,' he said patiently, running a hand through his hair. He looked rather tired, or maybe he just needed a shave. 'I only thought if we could put away a bit extra as long as you're working, it would come in useful.'

'No doubt.' I sat down and put my feet up.

'How long d'you think that'll be?'

'What?'

'That you're working.'

I shrugged. 'Entirely up to Mrs Whatsit. They say she'll be back some time in January. That's all I know.'

He frowned. 'Doesn't give us very long.'

'Well, we knew that when I started.'

'Yes, I know. D'you think we can save a bit more?'

'I don't know. If we don't go anywhere or do anything, I suppose so.'

'We might as well start,' Malcolm said. 'We'll have to manage when you stop work.'

This annoyed me. 'I don't see the logic of that. Why start practising? Why be miserable before we have to be? It's like saying you're going to die one day so you might as well die now.'

'No, it's not,' said Malcolm.

'It bloody well is,' I shouted.

The silence afterwards was devastating.

'Val, what's the matter?' he said eventually. He came and bent down beside my chair. 'What's bothering you?'

I shut my eyes till I saw brightness. 'Oh, nothing much,' I said. 'Everything's just fine.'

His voice was very quiet and gentle. 'I'm sorry you feel so bad about the baby. I'm sorry we haven't got more money. But there's nothing I can do.'

He was stroking my hair. I twitched my head away and tried to control my voice when I answered. 'I'm just tired,' I said. 'Tired and fat and depressed. That's all.'

95

He stood up. 'Can I do anything? What would you like to do?'

I considered this. 'Read, I think,' I said. I was halfway through *Tom Jones*. I picked it up.

'Oh yeah,' Malcolm said. 'I saw the film. It was good.'

I opened the book.

'All right,' he said. 'I'll get supper then, shall I?'

Christmas advanced inexorably. I became very aware of time. Like a river of blood and doom it was carrying me towards the beginning of April. The first of April, I hoped. It would serve it right.

I had always enjoyed Christmas with Mother and Jean, but this year it was different, spoilt. There were Malcolm's parents to visit as a duty. But, more than that, it marked the end of the year, a firm division. After that I would be sliding downhill, job gone, money gone, girth increasing. No escape. And a happy new year to all my readers.

I began to work feverishly to send Mrs Franklin my Fielding essay before Christmas. Milton had been quite well received, though it had taken her rather a long time to return my essays with her red biro comments attached. Even that gave me waves of nostalgia. I went on from *Tom Jones* to read extracts from three other Fielding novels.

Christmas paraphernalia filled the shops: cards and food and wrapping paper and an incredible assortment of bath cubes and talc specially boxed for the occasion. Chain stores overflowed with scarves ('Always so handy, don't you think, and you can just slip it in an envelope with the card,') and shoe shops sold out of their few remaining boots. It grew cold and foggy. I got fatter.

Jean was being secretive. 'Your present's going to be a surprise,' she said on one of her Sunday visits.

'Well naturally,' I said, 'unless you tell me what it is.'

'It's a secret.' She was hugging herself and swivelling round on the kitchen stool.

'All right, then don't tell me.'

'It's going to be a real surprise. But I'm sure you'll like it.'
'Good.'

She sighed, watching me with bright young eyes. I could feel her effort at self-control was nearly killing her.

'Tell me if you want to,' I said mischievously. She was the only person these days who could cheer me up.

'Oh no. That'd spoil it.' But she kept returning to the subject as if involuntarily and then leaping off it, suddenly, shocked by her own weak-mindedness.

Presently she started wandering round, fiddling with things, looking out of the window. 'Where's Malcolm?' she said at last.

'Out. Jeff came round.'

'Oh. Won't I see him?'

'Not unless you wait till he comes back.'

She drooped. 'I promised Mother I'd be back for tea.'

'Ring her up,' I suggested, 'and tell her you're staying.'

She looked tempted but sad. 'I can't really. She's making scones. I can't leave her to eat them all by herself.'

Quite suddenly I wanted to cry but I was afraid, apart from worrying Jean, that I might never stop.

'I hope I marry someone like Malcolm,' she said.

I swallowed hard. 'But not in such a hurry please, Jeanie.'

She frowned. 'You always say that. But I don't think it matters when you really love someone.'

'You're very romantic.'

She persisted. 'Well, does it? You're not sorry, are you? You're not sorry you got married?'

I had to smile and shake my head. Jean rocked perilously on the stool. 'I'm dying to be an aunt,' she said. 'How much longer is it?'

'Three months at least. Maybe a bit longer.'

'Oh. The end of next term, then.'

'Yes. More or less.'

'That's ages.' She considered it. 'How long before it can call me Auntie Jean?'

'Oh, God knows.' My resources were wearing thin. 'Years.' But she looked so disappointed I made another effort. 'Maybe not, though. Maybe it'll learn fast.'

One thing, however, became certain. At the library, just before we closed for the holiday, a cheerful, rosy, blue-eyed face surrounded by curly brown hair peeped round the door to be greeted with squeals of delight from Miss Mills and Sandra.

'Hullo,' it said to me. 'I'm Pat Carey. I'm so grateful to you for holding the fort. Can you hang on till the second week in January?'

TWENTY-TWO

A sort of quiet savagery possessed me by the time Christmas actually arrived. I felt very much part of the annual sacrifice, like the slaughtered turkeys, as I prepared to be festive. We were dividing the day between both families so as not to offend anyone. Our presents had been bought, out of funds, for about eight-and-sixpence each, not so much for suitability as price. We had sent cards to all who might expect them or, worse, send them to us. I wanted snow, but it didn't come, just a damp chill in the air and a kind of drabness. I felt more than ever before the contrast of the seasons and my life. Last June even, six months ago, how different! I almost believed that I would wake.

I chose to have lunch with Malcolm's parents so that I could leave to visit my mother. I wore a black sweater and the beautiful dark green velvet pinafore dress she had made me specially for Christmas. I would have loved it if I could have forgotten its purpose. I was beginning to feel I had been floating around in a tent for the whole of my life, yet the worst was to come.

Malcolm's mother called greetings from the kitchen and Malcolm's father issued us with glasses of dark, sweet sherry, with jokes about it not doing me any harm. We sat, and Malcolm made filial conversation about cars and television. I felt again like a child taken unwillingly out to tea in uncongenial company. The room was tiny, over-furnished and fussily decorated; my eyes were tired already from balloons and red ribbon and tinsel cards. There was a tiny pretend tree on top of the piano, which no one ever played, and fairy lights all over it.

One or two neighbours came in to say happy Christmas, swig sherry and glance ever so swiftly and tactfully at the middle of me to make sure I was still increasing and multiplying too fast for my wedding date. One of them had a dab of fat on her chin. That pleased me. Mrs Ross came in to talk to them.

'Hilda's holding the fort in the kitchen,' she said. I had forgotten Hilda, Malcolm's aunt, mother of the unpopular Connie who had had the good sense upon marriage to remove herself to Scotland, and who was spending Christmas with her husband's parents.

'That's nice,' the neighbours said. 'You'll be glad of a bit of help.'

'Well,' said Mrs Ross, 'she's all on her own now since Arnold passed away and it's not the same, is it?'

'No,' they agreed, 'you want to be with your own at Christmas. How about your mother, Valerie? Expect she misses you, doesn't she?'

'She's got Jean,' I said stiffly.

'Oh yes, of course. How old is she now?'

'Fourteen.'

'Fourteen, is she? Your mother'll have her hands full, then.' They beamed at me, evidently expecting some response. I said nothing. They appealed to Malcolm's mother. 'They grow up so fast these days don't they?'

'They certainly do.'

After some more chat they departed and there was only a brief lull before all five of us sat down to Christmas lunch, to the accompaniment of the peculiarly dismal brand of cheer provided by the wireless on most festive occasions. I was placed opposite Hilda, by whom I had been embraced. It wasn't long before I noticed that she ate with her mouth open. It wasn't pleasant to watch the food rolling inside, backed by rhythmic clicking of presumably loose false teeth. I pitied Hilda but I still wanted to cleave her skull.

'Here we are,' said Malcolm's mother. 'Another Christmas dinner. I always think I'll never get everything done in time. I like to be all washed up and sat down when the Queen comes on.'

'It can't be much of a Christmas for her, poor thing,' said Auntie Hilda, 'having to do a broadcast and be on the telly on Christmas Day.'

'Oh no, Hilda,' said Mrs Ross, 'she records it earlier on now, you know.'

'Does she?' Hilda said. 'I didn't know that.' She looked disappointed. 'Then it's not quite the same, is it?'

'No, but it does give her a proper family Christmas,' said Mrs Ross.

'I thought that was what you wanted, Hilda,' said Malcolm's father. 'Beer or cider?'

'What? Oh, cider please; you know I can't drink beer.'

He poured. 'And for you, love,' he added, addressing his wife, somewhere between question and statement. She was busily carving; apparently no else was allowed to attack her bird. I watched the stuffing being gouged out of the innards and thought how easily the wrong mood, the wrong company, could make something pleasant and ordinary become repulsive.

'How about you, Valerie?' He turned to me.

'Beer, please.'

'Oh. Going to join the men, are you?'

'Val doesn't like cider,' said Malcolm defensively.

'That's all right. We've got plenty of both. There's some Guinness if you'd rather, Malcolm.'

'No thanks, Dad. I'll have the same as Val.'

The carving finished and the vegetable dishes (brought out in honour of the occasion, for normally everything was dumped on the plates 'to save work') stopped moving across the table like syncopated chessmen. We all ate. Auntie Hilda, having started first after being admonished not to wait and let it get cold, was way ahead.

'Well,' said Malcolm's mother a trifle impatiently, 'is it all right?'

'Very nice, love.'

'It's fine, Mum.'

'We've done it again,' said Hilda with satisfaction. 'There's nothing like the old team.'

'Valerie?' Malcolm's mother turned to me. It seemed each of us must render tribute in turn, observe the ritual. I was embarrassed. There were no words left for me that would not sound false.

'It's lovely,' I said.

By the time we reached the Christmas pudding, black and sticky beneath its sprig of holly, I was exhausted by talk of friends and relatives I did not know. The fact that it was Christmas again seemed to provoke a flood of reminiscence about previous Christmases. I began to feel like Scrooge.

The pudding was served and custard poured over it. Strange, when you came to think of it, knowing what you would eat on a certain day each year for the whole of your life.

'Come on, Val, eat up,' said Mr Ross. 'You've got to eat for two remember.' He winked at me.

'No, she hasn't,' said Mrs Ross. 'It's not like that these days. Is it, Valerie?'

'No.'

Mrs Ross smiled brightly at her husband. 'So you see, you don't know everything,' she said, 'you men.'

Malcolm grinned at his father. 'That puts us in our place, eh, Dad?'

'Ah,' said his father, unperturbed. 'But where would they be without us? That's what I'd like to know.' They laughed.

'That'll be quite enough, thank you very much,' said Mrs Ross. It was hard to tell if the crossness was real or feigned.

'You eat your pudding. You know I want to get cleared away.'

Afterwards my offer of help was refused with the advice to sit down and put my feet up, and Auntie Hilda and Mrs Ross did the washing up while Malcolm and his father talked politics and I nearly interrupted to argue with them before remembering I was not expected to. When the others finally joined us we all ritually handed over and received our presents in a flurry of string and wrapping, as the transaction had to be completed before the Queen was upon us. When at last she began her survey of the year we all sat and paid attention in a kind of reverent silence that I suppose replaced church attendance, and I hoped she was having a better Christmas than I was. On my lap were Auntie Hilda's bath cubes and Mrs Ross's pink bedjacket ('to look pretty in hospital when Malcolm comes to see you').

After that we were stuck with the television which, coupled with the large meal and the unaccustomed drinking, soon induced sleep. I picked up the paper and found the usual choice of pantomime, circus, Christmas parties and old films for the rest of the day. Mr Ross was snoring gently. Auntie Hilda and Mrs Ross slept a little, then woke themselves up with small snuffling noises and looked round quickly to see if anyone had noticed. I flashed retreat signals at Malcolm, but he looked shocked. I withdrew to the kitchen, ran the cold tap, poured myself a glass of water and drank it very slowly.

Malcolm followed me. He came into the kitchen and stood behind me. 'Are you all right?'

'Sure.'

He put an arm round my shoulders. 'You sound fed up.' I looked out of the window at the back yard and the grey roofs of the opposite houses. The sky was leaden and the air had a raw look about it so that you knew without going outside how its texture would strike your skin.

'It's a funny sort of day,' I said.

'Never mind.' He went on holding me. 'Next year we'll stay at home if you like.' I said nothing, so he went on, 'Remember last year? What we were doing about now?'

'Yes,' I said. It was a year ago tomorrow that we had first really had sex, slightly carried away with drink. 'Looking forward to the party,' I said. It had been the start of this even though it had not in itself been fatal.

Malcolm turned me round and kissed me. 'Don't wish it had never happened,' he said.

'No.'

'We'll be all right.'

'Yes. Can we go soon?'

'Well.' He hesitated. 'In about half an hour if we make them some tea, we could go after that. Are you very fed up?'

'No,' I lied, 'but they don't need us here if they're asleep.'

'I know, but we can't just sneak off and leave them.'

'I suppose not.' It was odd to be imprisoned in the house, isolated, and not to be seeking out a place to make love. Odd, too, to spend so long on a visit, at a loose end. Before the wedding we had just dashed in and out, unless the house was empty, always on our way to something: a drive, a walk, a cinema. I turned my head away.

'What time did you tell your mother?' Malcolm asked.

'Any time after four.'

'Oh well, that's all right. She's probably asleep herself.'

'No.' My eyes stung. 'She'll be out walking with Jean.'

'Why? Is that what you always did?'

'Yes.' I went on looking out of the window. 'A long walk after lunch. We made up stories in turn as we went along and the next one had to take over.' The roof-tops were misty at the edges. 'We always left off at a really difficult part. And if there was snow we made a snowman.'

'Val,' said Malcolm, 'you're crying.'

My shoulders shook. Tears were rolling down my cheeks, but I wasn't making a sound.

'Oh love,' said Malcolm, 'what's the matter?'

'I don't know,' I said. I felt very stupid. Impossible to say that I was crying for my lost childhood, but those were the only words that came to mind.

'It's all right, Val,' said Malcolm, rocking me. 'I'll look after you.'

TWENTY-THREE

ON the doorstep my mother embraced us, then eyed me critically. 'Oh good,' she said. 'The frock's a success. I'm so glad.'

'It's marvellous,' I said.

She looked pleased. 'The line is just right,' she said with satisfaction, 'and I've always liked you in that colour.'

'It's only my favourite,' I said, and we smiled at each other.

'We had a marvellous walk,' Jean was saying to Malcolm. 'You and Val should have come. We found a pond with some ice on it, very thin ice, and we threw stones and cracked it. And we picked some twigs. We're going to paint them.'

'What was your story about?' I asked, trying to be casual.

'About a school. We've got a new special agent. He's a teacher in this school near the Berlin Wall and he's really helping refugees across and hiding them in the cloakrooms at night.'

I looked at my mother. 'Sounds good,' I said.

'It got very exciting in the later stages.'

Jean was showing Malcolm her Christmas presents. 'Look, I got all these records. Can we play them now? Will you dance with me if I put them on?'

Malcolm said, 'Sure.' He looked happy. Jean was very good for his ego, much better than I was lately. I was grateful to her.

'All right,' said my mother, 'but not too loud, Jean, and don't wear Malcolm out. Valerie and I will go in the dining-room.'

It was where I had done nearly all my studying and in

a way more full of memories than any other room in the house. The dining table was pushed back against the wall and we sank into deep, comfortable armchairs, very old and rather battered, in front of the fire.

'How did it go?' my mother asked.

I knew at once what she meant. 'Oh, I was bored stiff.'

'Was it as bad as that?'

I tried to be fair. 'Not really. They didn't do anything awful. I just felt out of place.'

'I do know the feeling,' my mother said. 'The first Christmas I spent with your grandparents, I remember looking at your father and wondering how he could possibly be their son. But they were perfectly nice to me. I was just being intolerant. I still am and evidently you've inherited it.' She took out cigarettes. 'Are you still smoking?'

'Yes please.'

We both had cigarettes. 'Hey,' I said, at a sudden thought, 'Jean's so excited she's forgotten presents.'

'Yes,' said my mother. 'I'm pleased really. I don't like her to think they're too important. We can have them later on.'

'They gave me a bedjacket,' I said.

'Did they? Well ... that was thoughtful.'

'Oh, Mother.'

Her lips twitched as I watched her. I dragged the garment out of its wrapping. 'It's revolting. Just look at it.'

It hung down, candy-floss pink and shapeless. Even its lacy holes seemed of varying sizes. It had ribbons at the neck.

'Well, they couldn't know,' said my mother, and then we both laughed. 'We're neither of us the bedjacket type, I'm afraid. Perhaps I've spent my life disappointing people by not giving them bedjackets. Presents are always a bit narcissistic, I think, however hard one tries.'

'I can't wear it,' I said.

'No. Well ...' She eyed it thoughtfully. 'No. Perhaps if

you know when they're coming to see you, you can slip it on just before they come and tear it off the minute they leave.'

'Tear it up more like.' I could feel my fingers vicious on it already. 'It's for hospital.'

'Yes.' She spoke casually, easily.

'I don't want to go.'

'Oh, I think it's the best place, for a first baby anyway. I had you at home, but nowadays they really prefer you to have a first baby in hospital. You won't be in long.'

'I mean I don't want to go anywhere. I don't want to have it at all.' I looked at the carpet, then upwards, straight at her, despairingly.

'Oh.' Her eyes took in a lot while she said nothing. 'Is that why you've been so quiet lately, the few times I've seen you?'

I nodded. It was strange, trying to find the relief of confidence without saying too much.

'It's not too bad,' she said. 'I won't tell you it doesn't hurt at all because it does, but there's nothing to get in a state over.' She spoke very calmly. 'And things have improved enormously since I had Jean.'

I said nothing. She added sharply, 'Has someone been telling you grisly stories?'

'No.'

'I should hope not. And, anyway, you'd surely have enough sense not to listen.'

'Oh yes.'

There was a pause. 'All right,' she said in a quiet, level voice. 'Let's have the rest of it.'

Given the chance, I was now not sure that I wanted to take it. 'Oh,' I said lightly. 'I don't think I shall be a very good mother. I haven't got any maternal feelings.'

'That's all right,' said my mother. 'You're not abnormal. Lots of women are like that.'

'And it works out?'

'Sorry,' she said at once. 'Why should you be interested

in lots of women? There's no reason why I shouldn't tell you. I was like that.'

I was startled. 'About me?'

'Yes.' She smiled. 'Please don't be offended. It didn't last more than about ten seconds after you were born. You see, I was always very selfish, more so when I was young, and your father absorbed me completely. I didn't want to share him with anyone. I didn't need anyone but him. But he wanted a family – daughters, as a matter of fact – and, well, it did work out.'

'Yes,' I said. 'It did.'

'You were such a success,' said my mother, 'that Jean was my own idea. And that really is a compliment.'

'I know,' I said. 'I'm glad you told me.'

'You see,' she said, 'when you're used to loving a person, an adult, it can be quite difficult to imagine loving somebody who doesn't exist yet and who won't be able to love you back for some time. Some women can imagine it easily. Others find it almost impossible. But this is no guide to which one makes the best mother when the child actually arrives.'

'No,' I said, 'I suppose not.'

'So there's no need to feel guilty,' she said.

'All right,' I said, 'then I won't,' and smiled at her.

I was too far gone; I had passed her. If the attitude we shared was a disease, she was only tainted, I was riddled through. It would be madness to display it all, just for the ease of saying everything, and lose her good opinion for which I had already sacrificed much.

'It really is a very absorbing job when you get down to it,' she said, 'and all part of the pattern, part of your marriage. That's why I didn't say too much to you about wasting your talents. We both know you missed an opportunity of going to university – all this could have come later – but that doesn't mean you haven't gained something as well.'

I said, 'I know'.

'And besides,' she added, 'looking back is very unprofitable.'

She had always been practical – it was something I loved about her – but not nearly so ambitious for me as I was for myself. She had accepted that I should go to university because I had the ability to get there. Any sacrifices she might have to make were incidental. But that was probably all. To me it was Mecca because it represented so many ambitions: not just studying a subject I loved but obtaining a degree that would make me independent in a way she had never been by giving me an earning capacity that could surmount disaster. Not just obtaining a degree but meeting people with my interests among whom I would find the one who made everyone else vanish. She had given me this ideal by achieving it. 'We used to sit up till three in the morning,' she said once. 'We must have talked about everything under the sun. I don't think I was really alive till I met your father.'

Knowing myself so well, and what I had wanted and why, I could excuse myself everything. But it was probably impossible to tell anyone's mother, let alone your own, that you hated your unborn child, and expect only sympathy and no revulsion. Reluctance, fear, lack of feeling could, if you were lucky, be accepted, but the violent physical loathing that I felt – no, unreasonable to ask anyone to take that in their stride. Unshared, though, it seemed to grow stronger.

Jean's gramophone, formerly mine, was still playing at moderate volume in the next room, an incongruous background for our conversation. The floor occasionally vibrated to the dancers' movements. I said cheerfully, 'Let's go and see how they're getting on.'

TWENTY-FOUR

In January I welcomed the cold that everyone else complained of. My job at the library was over, though all the inmates were kind and said repeatedly how pleased they would be to see me at any time in the future. Leaving the library made an enormous difference, one I had not been prepared for. I had expected mere poverty. This came, and though it was quite bad enough, I was more struck, because surprised, by the changed pattern of my life. Time was completely altered. Instead of a day hectic with work and travelling, meals and study, I now found vast areas of emptiness. I was in a desert of freedom; I had joined the army of housewives moving trance-like round the shops at times when they are not crowded. I could listen to wireless programmes I had never known existed. In school holidays I had always been so active, swimming, riding, playing tennis, or else reading books in the back garden that I scarcely switched on the radio. Now my body made nonsense of the fact that I had ever been energetic. Dressing and undressing was an ordeal to be got through quickly, almost with closed eyes, and for several months I had detested my daily bath because there was no way I could avoid the sight of my body and the contact I had to make with it. It was as if some monstrous joke had been played on me.

I was alone in the house, as I had never been before. There was silence. Everyone I knew was at work or at school. The telephone never rang and there was no one I could call on it. Only the BBC announcers talked to me and played music for me, this heavy, unknown young woman in her empty flat, mechanically dusting and washing up. It should have been ideal because in theory I could please myself. I could dash merrily through my shopping and housework and have as much time as I liked for reading. In practice I found I did chores slowly or not at all, and could no longer read indiscriminately. I tried Restoration comedy, but the jokes about sex had a hollow sound. I sought refuge in Jane Austen, but her enchantments were dimmed: I had forgotten how relentlessly her heroines chase men. Swift was my deliverer: his disgust at mankind, moral and physical, was as invigorating as the January air.

So I worked, but more slowly than before. I seemed to have less energy and found it harder to concentrate for long periods. I had to take ten-minute breaks more often, during which I wandered round the flat and looked at things. Jean's Christmas present lay in a drawer all by itself: a baby's dress, painstakingly made with love and extreme difficulty. Knowing this, when I received it, had brought tears to my eyes, which she luckily interpreted as maternal pleasure. I still wanted to cry now, as I touched it. The thought of Jean, who hated sewing even more than my mother and I did, who could scarcely manage to thread a needle, labouring for weeks to produce this garment was almost more than I could bear. I wondered how many times she had had to unpick it.

One afternoon when I was very tired and deeply involved with Swift, Malcolm's mother arrived.

'I was just passing,' she said, 'so I thought I'd pop in and see you.'

I considered this unpardonable since the invention of the telephone, so I merely said, 'Come in,' and 'Sit down,' and 'I'll put the kettle on,' not rudely but without expression. When I returned to the room she peered into my face. 'Are you all right, love?' she asked, but I sensed curiosity rather than warmth. 'You look a bit drawn.'

I shrugged slightly. 'I'm okay.'

'You must take care of yourself, you know. Do you get your feet up every afternoon?'

'Oh yes,' I said. 'They were up when you came.'

'That's right,' she said calmly. She reached into her bag and produced a knitting pattern which she waved under my nose. 'How do you like this?'

It was a matinée jacket, apparently, whatever that means, rather sickeningly displayed not merely alone but as worn by a bald baby with a very large head and an empty expression. Luckily, because speech was quite beyond me, she answered her own question.

'Isn't it sweet?' she said. 'I thought I'd do it in white. Or would you rather have lemon? I dressed Malcolm all in white at first till I'd got some things in blue. I wouldn't have blue or pink before he was born, not knowing. But you can have lemon if you'd rather.'

I said faintly, 'I don't mind.'

She appeared satisfied. 'Then I'll do it in white, I think. I didn't like to get the wool till I'd seen you. I should've started before really, but what with Christmas and that ... And anyway, I don't like to start too soon, just in case.'

A pity, I thought. A touch of voodoo or whatever might have helped.

'Now you must tell me,' she said as if it mattered, 'how much you've done yourself. I don't want to barge in if there's something you'd rather do yourself.'

'Nothing.'

Mrs Ross said, 'Pardon.'

I repeated, 'Nothing.' I tried to simplify. 'I don't knit.'

It took her a moment to gather breath. 'But everyone knits when they're expecting a baby. It's not difficult.'

I shook my head. 'I don't want to knit.'

There was a pause. I thought for a second she was going to challenge me and I was almost afraid of what I might say, but she didn't. Obviously too monstrous a thought that I was a resentful, reluctant, *unnatural* mother-to-be. Better a freak too lazy to knit.

'Oh,' she said in a sharper tone, 'very well, then. It's up to you. I'll just go ahead then, shall I?'

'Yes, if you like,' I said, adding, 'Thank you.'

She replaced the pattern in her handbag. 'Well,' she said, 'what have you been doing with yourself, then?'

The kettle screamed and I got up. When I returned with the tray she had *Gulliver's Travels* in her hand.

'Oh,' she said questioningly, 'school books?'

'Not exactly,' I said. We looked at each other, a cold, searching look. 'Just books.'

She almost sniffed. A muscle in her face twitched, not quite raising an eyebrow. 'So that's why you've not had time to knit,' she said. 'Too busy ... reading.' She made the word sound very nearly obscene.

I kept my voice calm. 'I didn't say I hadn't time to knit,' I reminded her. 'I said I didn't want to knit.'

Again the keen look, but this time a fencer's eye, getting the measure of an opponent. As my dislike for her increased, so did my respect.

'So you'd rather read,' she said at last.

'That's right.'

She said with satisfaction, 'Well, you won't have time for reading when you've got a baby to look after.'

The whole scene had a bizarre quality. We were still, very largely, speaking in polite tea-time voices, but the tray lay untouched between us.

'You want to come down off your high horse, young lady,' she said. 'You've got nothing to be so high and mighty about.'

'Have you said that to Malcolm?'

'He knows how I feel. You like to think you're too good for him, but you were glad enough to take his name.'

We were speeding up now. I could feel my anger mounting and with it a mixture of fear and exhilaration. She must have hated me for a long time.

'I hadn't the heart to refuse,' I said. 'He was so pressing.'

She flushed. 'You know what I mean. He's a decent boy and he stood by you. And that's more than you deserve.'

I said, 'Would you rather your grandchild was born a bastard?'

She flinched at the language and it spurred her on. 'I'd like to be sure it is my grandchild.'

I was taken aback, and admiring. 'You should ask Malcolm. He seems pretty sure.'

'He's soft.' She made a scornful, pitying sound. 'He's daft about you.'

This assessment of the situation nearly startled me off the main track. She took her chance to go on. 'It turns me over to see you making a fool of him.'

I felt strange now in my head. In a sense we were arguing on one level while the words represented quite another and more intuitive layer of feeling. She had hit on some partial truth and without any real evidence to lead her there. I felt sure, also without proof, that there was a large element of sexual jealousy in her antagonism and this put me, however savage her thrusts, into a basically superior position.

'I'm not making a fool of him,' I said. 'He's got what he wanted.'

'Maybe he'll soon get tired of it,' she said. 'Easy come, easy go.'

'Oh, I don't think so,' I said slowly. I looked at her not as a heavily pregnant woman but with eyes that remembered things she didn't want to think about. Psychologically she had a very slimming effect. I had not felt so glamorous for months.

'There's more to marriage than just catching a husband,' she said. 'You think you're very clever but you've got a lot to learn.'

'If I want to.'

'Oh, it's all self with you,' she stormed. 'Let me tell you, my girl, marriage is all give and take and when you've got a baby to look after you won't have time to sit reading. It's time you got down to a bit of work and made a proper home for my son.'

It was the proprietary words 'my girl' that blinded me. I stood up. 'I think you've said enough,' I said. 'You're a guest here and I didn't invite you. It's none of your business what I do with my time, now or later. If you think Malcolm's getting a raw deal, tell him not me.'

She was also standing now, breathing rather hard but saying nothing. She looked startled, and I wondered for the first time how far the momentum of the whole thing had carried her along.

'There's no need to bring him into it,' she said as if I had threatened her. 'We've both said a lot of things that's maybe best forgotten.'

'You have a very convenient memory,' I said. 'Why should you come in here and insult me and then tell me to forget it all?'

'All right,' she said heavily. 'Maybe I said too much. Not that it wasn't true,' she added, a strange peace manoeuvre, 'but I said more than I should. It can't do any good to –'

'Then it's a pity you said it,' I interrupted.

'You said a lot too, don't forget,' she said promptly.

'Well, naturally.'

Again a pause. I was oddly embarrassed, faced with this large, plain woman with whom I had had much too frank a conversation.

'Perhaps it was bound to come,' she said at last in a peculiarly resigned way. 'We haven't got much in common and I must admit you wouldn't have been my choice for Malcolm. And you've made it pretty clear I'm not your ideal mother-in-law. Well, we've both bottled a lot up. Maybe it's better out and we can start afresh.'

I had to respect her. There was even a kind of reason in

what she said, although she was presumably hoping to persuade me, without actually asking, not to tell Malcolm what had happened. I wanted time to think.

'Maybe,' I said. 'We'll have to see.'

She went slowly, almost reluctantly, as if she might think of something worth adding if she lingered. Her expression was a mixture of hostility and conciliation. We were both embarrassed by the scene we had shared.

On the step she paused and remarked, 'Well, we've both had our say. Maybe we can let bygones be bygones now.' Her eyes looked past mine.

I said, 'Yes. Perhaps.'

It was only after she had gone that I realized how tired I was.

TWENTY-FIVE

MALCOLM found me slumped in a chair when he came in. He thought I was reading and peered over my shoulder.

'What's that, *Gulliver's Travels*? That's kids' stuff, isn't it?'

'Not exactly.'

He looked at me more closely. 'Are you okay? You look all in.'

'I've had a busy day,' I told him.

'What you been doing? Or is that a hint you want me to get supper?'

'No. Can't you just sit down for a minute?'

'Sure.' He sat, looking suddenly pleased. 'What's up, honey? Is my baby lonesome?'

'Oh don't,' I said. 'Malcolm, did your parents object to our getting married? Really object, I mean.'

His expression became embarrassed and evasive. 'Why? What's brought this up?'

'You should have told me,' I said.

'Told you what?'

'That they really objected. After my mother saw them she said they'd taken it very well.'

He frowned. 'Yeah. Well, they did.'

'But only in front of her.'

He was silent.

'Is that what you mean?'

He took out cigarettes. 'Look, Val, what's brought this up? Has someone been talking to you?'

'I want to know.'

'Well, so do I. Why are you suddenly asking all this now?'

'Your mother came round today,' I said, 'and I got the impression she's not too crazy about me.'

He seemed relieved. 'Well, that's nothing new.'

'No, more than that. So I started wondering. Did they say a lot to you they didn't say to my mother?'

He shrugged. 'Oh well, they went on a bit. You know.'

'No, I don't,' I said. 'You didn't tell me. And I wish you had.'

'Why? It didn't make any odds.'

'It can't have been pleasant.'

'No. Well, you know how parents go on. They get a bit worked up. They don't mean it.'

'How bad was it?'

'Oh, not bad.'

'Malcolm, I really want to know.'

'Look, Val, what's Mum been saying?'

I shook my head. 'Nothing much. We were just two women having a cat session. But I got the impression she thought I wasn't much of a wife for you; too much reading, not enough cooking and knitting, that kind of thing.'

I watched him closely. His face darkened and he said in a quiet yet somehow frightening voice, 'She ought to mind her own bloody business.'

I was shaken but I said calmly, 'I don't want you to have a fight with her.' There was no point that I could see in repeating our conversation, and I felt there was some degree of justice in part of what she had said. 'We've never got on well and we let off some steam. I just want to know about the wedding. Did you have a row?'

Malcolm was up and walking about the room. Standing with his back to me, looking out of the window and smoking rapidly, he said, 'Yeah, we had a row. We had a row every night for about two weeks. But they knew they couldn't stop me, so it was just a bloody waste of time.'

He had never even hinted at this. I felt humble yet indescribably laden, as with a real weight. My mind moved on to another area.

'Did you get teased at work?' I asked.

'Oh well, you always get that,' he said easily.

There was silence while I considered in some detail the various crudities that the home and the bank had probably employed. They must have had plenty of scope. Ours was such an old and classic situation.

'I'm sorry,' I said. But I was resentful, too. I didn't want to be the object of sacrifice, to be shielded from the truth, put before everyone. It was unequal. I was not offering enough in return. I thought he had understood that when he made our agreement. Now it was as if he had broken the rules in secret.

'That's all right,' he said, turning round from the window. Against the light I could not see his face clearly. 'What does it matter?'

'I wish you'd told me,' I said. But this was inadequate when what I meant was: don't give me more than I can accept.

TWENTY-SIX

PEOPLE say there is growth all the time, that no relationship can be static. I had not been aware of this with Malcolm: we had gone on as before, more or less. I had not been trying to develop anything; I was too conscious of the limitations of our marriage and I had other things on my mind. But now I was alerted, suspicious. Not constantly, of course, but recurrently, as a tongue returns to probe a sore place.

Tiny pieces of evidence, formerly unnoticed, swam back into my mind with new significance, like the images and voices that swirl through mist round the hero's head in an old film when he and the audience have to be reminded of something important that they have forgotten. I was using a sort of do-it-yourself flashback kit. I was surprised how much material there was, once I started looking. Unreasonable tolerance, surprising tenderness, willingness to help, lack of criticism, increasing interest ... I had to stop it; it was too alarming. Malcolm had been and was being far too good to me, beyond the ordinary call of duty. I could compose a citation for him. Or I could report him to the Committee for Unacceptable Activities. Did he know he was living in a police state and that I was the police?

We had saved about sixty pounds from my job and it reposed in the post office. I had never considered money very much before, but now, in our present circumstances, it gave me a distinctly odd feeling to realize that, apart from Malcolm's (inadequate) salary, this was all the money we had in the world. I wondered how long it would last, what we would do with it.

In the evening now Malcolm did not often play records or watch television, and he hardly ever went out with Jeff. He sat doing sums on the backs of envelopes, while I read or watched him. Sometimes I felt too sleepy – drugged, almost – to work. It was hard to get comfortable in my chair, though, so I couldn't really rest.

'I don't see how we can manage on this,' he said one night. 'Take away the rent and we haven't got enough to live on. Less than you used to earn.'

'I know,' I said. I couldn't see the point of stating this dismally obvious fact.

'How are you finding it?' he asked with interest, as if there was something we could do about it.

'Well,' I said, 'I didn't deposit any of my last pay-packet, so that helped but it's all gone now, of course.'

'And things are tight for you? Shopping and that?'

'Yes.' I couldn't think why he was so keen to hear the worst. 'Naturally. Haven't you noticed how dull the food is?' It made me feel worse just to admit it. Very shortly I would be joining the other housewives in a morning chat on how money didn't go anywhere, did it, and prices always went up, never down. I would go home comforted and make nourishing soups from bones.

'Oh, the food's all right,' he said cheerfully. 'I think you manage very well. But you're bound to feel the pinch. We used to spend half your money, didn't we?'

'About that,' I said. Sometimes I had cheated.

'I think we should move,' Malcolm said.

I sighed and shut my eyes, wishing my stomach didn't feel so uncomfortable. 'Where to? There aren't any cheaper flats that are big enough.'

'But this one is too expensive.'

'Yes,' I said, 'and I told you that before we took it.'

'I know. But it's been all right so far and we knew it would be. Now it's making things rather tight. It'll be years before you can work again, so we'd better plan ahead. I think we should try to buy a house.'

I opened my eyes. 'What with?'

'With a loan from the bank.' He looked at me triumphantly and passed me one of his envelopes. 'I can get quite a good loan. See how it works out. We'd be quite a bit better off.'

I looked. 'Yes,' I said. 'The mortgage is less than the rent.' That was the only improvement I could see. I looked again at the weekly expenditure. 'You've forgotten petrol,' I said.

He shook his head. 'No car.'

'What? Oh Malcolm, we've had this before. What's the point –?'

He interrupted, a shade grimmer than the last time this had been discussed. 'The point is, saving tax and insurance for a start. And getting some cash. We're going to need some deposit and a bit of furniture, however cheap.'

The car had been the passport to so many of our happiest times that I felt it was terribly unlucky to part with it. I put this another way. 'But you love the car,' I said.

He didn't look at me; he was scribbling on another bit of paper. 'It's only a car,' he said. 'It's stupid to keep it if we'd be better off without it. Anyway, suppose something goes wrong with it that I can't fix. We can't afford to have it done.'

'We've got sixty pounds.'

'No.' He sounded very firm. 'We mustn't touch that. That's for the baby, for whatever we don't get from our parents, and emergencies.'

I laughed. 'Let's hope we don't have too many emergencies.'

'Well, now do you see my point?'

The conversation revived all the other times we had discussed money. It made me feel that they all stretched out in a line, each more sickening than the last, like the apparitions in *Macbeth*. It seemed, whenever we talked money, that we had done nothing but talk money for the past six months.

I said, 'Yes, I see your point.' I looked again at the envelope. 'Is this the most you can borrow?'

He looked almost crestfallen. 'I'm afraid so. It's better than we'd get with a building society.'

I could imagine very clearly the sort of box and the sort of neighbours it would buy. 'It won't buy much of a house,' I said.

Malcolm said, 'Look, Val, if we could borrow more there'd be no point because the repayments would be as bad as the rent here, or worse. Now there's no sense in that, is there?'

'No.' He could have no idea how trapped and hunted all this made me feel: as if I was struggling under a huge net that had been thrown over me. 'What about a cheaper flat?' I attempted. This was quite hopeless and illogical and I knew it. I didn't know why I'd said it except the idea of a cheap and nasty house repelled me so much that anything seemed worth saying.

'We tried that before,' said Malcolm predictably. 'And you just said it's not possible.'

'I know.' We were going round in circles and I felt almost physically dizzy. I shut my eyes again and the next thing I knew Malcolm was crouching on the floor beside me. 'Cheer up, bird,' he said. 'I'll fix it. Leave it to wonder-boy.'

For a second I caught a flash of the old glamour which had so absorbed me; the vivid colouring and lush features, the dramatic quality of face and build. Gone quickly. So much for life with me, as husband and father-to-be. You take the one thing you like and ruin it.

'Okay,' I said, 'but there's something I can't leave to you.' I heaved myself out of the chair (it really was becoming that kind of effort) and went into the lavatory, the ultimate refuge. Outside, left alone in the sitting-room, Malcolm was whistling softly.

TWENTY-SEVEN

MEANWHILE we economized. I persuaded Malcolm not to do anything about the car without telling me, but he insisted on 'looking at houses' in the paper although we had more or less agreed that weather, time, and my state would make a move impossible before the birth. I was not at all resigned to moving but at least I had a reprieve. So I was quite free to concentrate on the game of stretching the pennies. There was high competition amongst goods in the shops to get on my list; it was fast becoming an elimination contest. I thought that I might not have minded this if I had chosen it freely, but, as it was, I could not forget that it might have been avoided. I could laugh at myself even while I resented becoming a comic figure. I used to watch myself peering into my purse and juggling the contents. I thought the cuteness of the picture wore off rather quickly.

Malcolm decided to give up smoking, or at least to cut down (he was not sure yet which), so I had the additional pleasure of watching him trying to ration himself. I had not chosen to give up and he said it didn't matter, as I smoked less than he did and it would be a bad time to choose for me to give anything up. However, the result of his sacrifice was that I felt guilty about smoking in front of him. It became ridiculous : I would postpone the cigarette that I wanted when he wasn't smoking, and have the cigarette that I didn't want as soon as he lit up. Ironically, in the day, when I was alone and free to smoke, I seldom wanted to. I was driven to the ultimate idiocy of wishing that we were both heavier smokers so that we could gain more by giving it up.

Early in February I finished my Swift essay and tramped through snow to post it to Mrs Franklin. It crossed with a letter from her saying that she couldn't do any more marking for a month because of mock GCE, which I was sure to remember. I had forgotten completely. Her world, her life and her year might be proceeding normally, but for me all time meant was that I got bigger and the weather got colder. Her letter, theoretically reasonable though it was, came as a slap in the face, like the Red Cross refusing to continue supplies to an internment camp. It seemed all the more unfair because Swift, though my most congenial subject so far, had cost me more in will-power and physical effort than the others, simply because I was slower now in everything that I did. Sometimes work that I really wanted to do was an ordeal, like climbing a high mountain without oxygen. But I was increasingly attracted to the eighteenth century. It was comparatively fresh, as we seemed to have concentrated on both earlier and later periods at school, and I was fascinated by the idea, however imperfect in practice, of an age of reason. I found I was reading history of the period to complement the literature I had studied, and developing the time sense that had been awakened in the sixth form. For years at school knowledge is compartmented and you don't believe the edges will ever merge until they do.

I felt remote now, as though I had always been pregnant. I could have given talks on *Living with my Disability*. My new detachment rather alarmed me; it was brought to my attention one night in bed. Malcolm started to make love to me and I realized, dimly at first, incredulously, like someone who finds that a limb is missing, that I felt no excitement, no desire, nothing. Malcolm was moving urgently and I could remember exactly what my response would have been. But I had never pretended in my life; I had never had to.

Malcolm said, 'What's up?'

I didn't know. I said, 'I'm too fat. I feel awful.' Any words would do while I tried to understand this strange deadness.

'Try another way,' Malcolm suggested.

We tried, but I must have shown reluctance because he stopped suddenly. 'I'm sorry,' he said, 'but it *is* a long time.'

I said, 'Yes'. I had not realized. There seemed to have been so much to think about. Even now my head was full up, as swollen as the rest of me. I felt there was a problem for me to solve, that I was fitting together the pieces of a jigsaw.

'Play another game?' Malcolm asked, but I lay still, my brain ticking over in my numb body. 'Okay, never mind,' he said presently. 'You're bound to feel a bit off now and then.' He lay with an arm round me and I half turned away to settle into sleep, but I could feel him against me, all ready and trying so hard not to be. In a moment he would turn over and be alone with that feeling. I could still remember it, though at the moment I could not feel it; remember it enough to know it should not be inflicted on anyone.

I waited a little, then turned round. 'Come on,' I said. 'I've changed my mind. But go easy. I'm a bit fat and fragile.' I was grateful, for the first time, that it was dark.

He was very gentle, as I had never asked him to be before. Everything seemed slower. Occasionally he asked me, 'Sure I'm not hurting you?' and I said, 'No, no.' I was a total observer; presently he was too lost to say anything. It brought home to me how much he had wanted to make love; my lack of response did not disturb him. Perhaps he was satisfied that it was a normal stage in pregnancy. Then at the last he got terribly excited, and I felt, ridiculous though it sounds, that I should not be there. He said, 'Oh Val, darling,' a second before the end, and the flooding sensation that usually thrilled me right through meant nothing. I was so sorry that I kissed him and he kissed me back, hard, then buried his face in my neck. He didn't make any jokes about success; in fact he didn't talk at all. I lay awake for hours, but he went to sleep quite quickly, holding me.

TWENTY-EIGHT

THEN he brought home a book on childbirth. I was reading Sitwell's life of Pope, to whom I had turned after Swift, and feeling that we both, though misshapen in different places, had quite a lot in common, when I looked up and saw Malcolm engrossed not in James Bond or envelope finance but in this unlikely book.

I said, 'What are you doing with that?' We had not discussed the other night; in fact we were more casual than ever.

He looked up, half-pleased to be caught. 'Doing my homework.'

'Whatever for?'

He put the book down and his hand strayed for a second to the cigarette packet before he remembered. 'I want to know what it's all about, and you never tell me much, so I thought I might as well read it up. I don't want to be dead ignorant about it all.'

I said flippantly, 'Why not? I am.'

'Not really. Anyway, I'm just curious.'

He returned to the book, but it took me a while to rejoin Pope in Twickenham. I felt more enmeshed than ever. I had in fact read books on childbirth because I wanted to know what to expect, but I wished, unreasonably no doubt, that Malcolm would not try to share this without being invited. Not that he was stealing a valuable experience, but there was an element of impertinence, as if I had found him spying on me in the lavatory. I began to shiver. Somehow, just because we had agreed to get married, we had become more and more exposed to each other, more naked. Books on child-birth, available to all, were like nude pictures of me. I needed my remoteness. I needed a refuge, an aim, a solution. I did not know what I meant. Was I going mad? I could not remember whether people had really said that those who doubt their sanity are always sane. Perhaps this was merely a fallacy lovingly preserved by the insane.

Surely there was somewhere I could go where everything would become simple. The small room, Malcolm and his book, the progress of the past months, all moved in to press and suffocate me as the ceiling descends in some horror films. I was silently having hysterics, like internal bleeding. It was terribly serious, only no one could tell, so there was no chance of treatment.

'It's fascinating,' Malcolm said. 'I wish I'd read it up before.'

I said, 'Good,' in what I hoped was a neutral tone.

Presently he said, 'Hey, we took some awful chances.'

'What do you mean?' But I knew what he meant.

'Earlier on. It says – ' he put on a quoting voice – 'you should "abstain from marital relations during the first ten weeks of pregnancy". Did you know that?'

It would have been safe and peaceful to say no. Instead I gave in to some demon. 'Yes, I knew that.'

He lowered the book. 'And you wanted to risk it? I wouldn't have, if you'd told me.'

'I know,' I said.

He looked uncertain. 'Well, thanks for the compliment.'

'You're welcome,' I said, 'but I wouldn't have minded if I'd lost the baby.'

There was a moment's silence. Then he said, 'D'you really mean that?'

I was quite calm, not vicious. 'Yes.'

He said in an offended tone, 'I wish I'd known that was what you were trying to do.'

'It wasn't just that,' I said. 'Don't be silly. I just thought it would be convenient if it happened anyway. You must admit it would have been.'

He looked at me with concern. 'I can't. Not any more. Not since I felt it moving.'

I looked away. He had made a great fuss about this the first few times it happened. It had embarrassed me and I had tried to forget it.

'It's got . . . sort of real to me,' he went on. 'Like a person. In less than two months it'll be *here*.' He even said the word with a touch of reverence and wonder.

'So it will,' I said.

'We ought to be thinking of names.'

'You said that months ago.'

'Well?' He seemed puzzled. 'All the more reason to get moving now.'

I said, 'Why?' and shifted in my chair, trying to get comfortable.

'Because we haven't got long. It'll have to have a name, won't it?'

'I suppose so.' I let too much expression get into my voice. 'All right, go ahead and think of some.'

Malcolm said sharply, 'Don't you *care*?'

I let myself be cruel. 'I told you before. If you had a grain of sensitivity you'd shut up about it.'

To my surprise and alarm he didn't get angry. 'I thought it'd get better,' he said.

'Well, it hasn't,' I said crisply. I felt a sudden influx of energy. 'D'you want me to tell you exactly how I feel about this baby?'

People should not answer this sort of question; it carries its own answer, which they should recognize. But Malcolm said, 'Yes. Tell me.'

I took a deep breath. I had expected to hurl the words but instead I spoke quietly. 'I don't want it. It doesn't mean a thing to me except as a damn nuisance. I hate it. I wish it

130

was dead. In fact I hope it dies so I won't have to bloody well look after it.'

'Don't say that.' Malcolm cut in on me. I had frightened myself, though I tried not to show it. 'You don't mean it,' he went on. 'I'm sorry, I know it's awful for you. You're under an awful strain. But I'm sure you'll feel differently when it's born. It says here nearly all women do.'

'Great,' I said. 'Thanks a lot.'

'Oh no,' he said. 'I didn't mean it like that. But I'm so sure you'll feel all right about it. It's probably quite normal to feel upset now.'

'I'm not worried,' I said, 'about being abnormal.'

Again he went on, undeterred. 'No, I mean you've had more to give up than me. Going to college and that. But I'm sure it'll work out when the baby's here. Look, Val – ' he became more earnest, an expression and tone quite at variance with his features, Casanova turned wet-nurse – 'I'll help you. I'll look after it so you can go out. You can go to evening classes if you like. I won't just sit back and leave you to do everything.'

Anger left me; I just felt tired and hopeless. I was defeated and far removed from the scene of battle. He was draining every vestige of colour from our life, leaving total grey. The pity I felt was like the scent of death.

'Thanks,' I said. 'I'm sure you won't.'

TWENTY-NINE

THAT night I could not sleep. I had had only occasional difficulty before, apart from the odd half hour spent shifting
position, but this was the real thing.

Malcolm slept quietly, breathing steadily beside me. He
seldom moved once he was asleep. I lay with my eyes wide
open and looked at the darkness and the objects in the room
that I could faintly make out. Presently I sat up and moved
the curtain so I could see through the window. There was
bright moonlight, softened now and then by clouds blowing
across the moon. The trees were moving rapidly. On the
ground something glittered like frost.

I lay down again but I was more awake than ever. I was
not consciously thinking: it was as if my mind was a computer which had been programmed and left to tick over. I
was restless with an activity that I did not have to control.

Time is almost impossible to measure while you lie awake
in darkness. When I sat up again to look at my watch by
moonlight, half an hour had passed. It could have been an
hour or ten minutes. I looked out of the window again and
I wanted to be out there.

The plan seemed quite normal, but I knew I must be careful about executing it. I stayed sitting up till I was cold, and
Malcolm did not stir. I stood up cautiously, balancing against
the wall, and stepped in two awkward movements off the
bed. Malcolm moved, turning over partially into the space
I had left, but his breathing was still quite regular. I groped
in the dark for my huge warm dress and slipped it on over
my nightdress. I muffled the door-handle in underclothes

before I turned it, and I left it wedged open behind me because this was safer and easier, and also a way of checking that Malcolm was still asleep.

I put on no lights. In the bathroom I found a pair of socks to wear in my winter boots and I put a coat over my dress. I had a sense of adventure I had not really experienced since midnight feasts with Marianne when we were both twelve. I slipped my key into my coat pocket and crept downstairs to the front door, feeling safe now from waking Malcolm but worried lest I disturb the people below into believing I was a burglar.

The front door was cooperative and success nearly made me careless with the front gate. Once on the pavement I was exhilarated and wanted to run but I was too bulky to do it properly. I registered this as a fact but I did not, for once, feel bulky. I felt light and energetic. Everywhere looked very exciting, quite unlike its daytime self. I had always loved driving at night, too, for the same reason and I wished now that I had done more of it, as if it was already too late.

I thought I was walking aimlessly, but presently I found myself alongside the children's playground and wanting desperately to go in. It was not locked, nor was the apparatus bolted down, as in some parks. The metal of the slide shone silver-grey and hard; the steps leading to it were in shadow. I gave a swing a push and it stopped drifting in the wind and moved backwards and forwards rhythmically at my touch. I felt liberated : I was doing something crazy and pointless and fun. I gave the roundabout a shove and it began to move, ponderously, rather like me.

There was a sandpit for younger children and I bent down and picked up a handful of sand. It was so cold. It seemed very strange, when sand evokes summer and warmth by the sea, that it should be cold, but this was sand long separated from sea-water, homesick sand lying in a large wooden trough and idly caressed by a pregnant young woman who hoped a policeman would not walk past. The feel of it on my hand was beautiful and satisfying. I let it drift away very slowly through my fingers.

When I stood up I noticed that the swing had nearly stopped moving. I must have spent as much time pushing Jean on swings as using them myself. When I was fourteen and she was nine, only she was theoretically entitled to rides, but I sneaked many, with Jean as look-out. Now I wanted another one.

I looked round from habit, but there was no one in sight on the grass hard with frost, or near the bushes at the edge of the ground. It was very cold. I took hold of the swing and the metal burnt my hands. I had forgotten gloves but I did not care. I lowered myself carefully onto the wooden seat, a tightish fit now, and edged back my feet for take-off. The moment of swinging forward gave an almost orgasmic pleasure. I held my feet straight out in front of me for maximum thrust and let my head fall back. The wind whipped my hair and I looked up into stars.

I swung for a long time even after I was breathless with excitement and the effort of maintaining the motion. I was alone in the best way. I didn't feel fat or pregnant or married. I was myself. Everything became possible.

I talked to myself, half aloud, half in my head: You're free; you can go. When this is over, born, finished, you can begin again. You have a right to life. Why bury yourself alive? You are free *now*, at this moment. Why not all the time?

The reasons clicked out of the computer: it will create less suffering in the long run if you go. So many people will love the child; let them take care of it. Better surely than being loathed by its mother. Why stay? You can do nothing but evil: torment the child, despise Malcolm, disappoint your mother and Jean, and in doing all this make yourself entirely wretched. There was no point in any of it.

I went on swinging. The trees rushed downwards as I swung towards them; the freezing air burned my face. I felt like a prisoner on the run or animal loosed from the zoo.

Anything was possible. Escape. A new life. Or even the old life I thought I had lost. Somewhere there could still be a miracle.

When I got off the swing I was dizzy and my hands frozen into a holding curve. I eased them straight gradually while I regained equilibrium, leaning against the post of the swing. I did not feel I had found a new plan; it had been there all along, it seemed now, like a parcel waiting to be opened. I walked home calmly and slowly, rejuvenated.

THIRTY

I was so sure I had been successfully quiet that it was a real shock to see a light on upstairs when I returned to the house. As I opened the front door, Malcolm's head appeared over the banisters. He looked worried, angry, and relieved.

'There you are,' he said accusingly.

I closed the door and said, 'Yes, here I am.' I climbed the stairs rather slowly. He watched me all the time.

'Where *have* you been?'

I didn't want another scene. If I was going to leave him in two or three months I might as well be pleasant in the meantime. A time limit makes any ordeal easier to bear.

'I felt like some fresh air,' I said. 'I thought you were asleep or I'd have told you.'

'You could have left a note,' he said, 'in case I woke up. You've been gone nearly an hour.'

I looked at my watch and thought, Longer, if you only knew. But I said, 'So I have. I didn't realize.' I warmed myself by the fire he had put on in the sitting-room.

He watched me in silence for a while before he said, 'Whatever were you doing?'

On this point I was determined. 'Just walking. I felt restless.'

Again a silence while he studied me. 'You must be frozen,' he said eventually.

'Only my hands really. I forgot my gloves.'

'Can I get you some tea? I've made some.'

'Yes,' I said. 'That would be nice.'

While he was gone I peeled off my coat and boots, and

sat in a chair before the fire. I felt very calm. He brought the tea in an earthenware mug. I drank.

'Is it all right?'

'It's fine,' I said. It was dark brown and very hot and sweet. 'Aren't you having any?'

'Oh, I've had gallons.' He looked shamefaced. 'I've been drinking it ever since I woke up.' He glanced around, a cigarette-hunting look, before remembering he hadn't got any. 'Val, while you were out, I was thinking. I'm sorry we had that fight.'

'So am I,' I said. After all, why not?

'I think – ' he hesitated – 'I think maybe I haven't always made allowances for how you are, being easily upset. I mean, we've talked about it but I haven't always remembered properly, to make allowances.' He was struggling. 'D'you see what I mean?'

'Yes,' I said.

'Well, I'm sorry.'

'That's all right,' I said. 'I've been pretty bitchy myself.'

'Maybe, but that's understandable, isn't it? I mean, you've got an excuse.' His dark hair was tousled from bed and he needed a shave, but despite this he looked most attractive. I could see it now with complete detachment. 'But I haven't. I shouldn't have gone on at you.'

I smiled. 'Maybe you won't have to again. I'll try to be more like a human being.'

'No –'

I interrupted. 'You don't want me to be human?'

He laughed. He hadn't laughed much lately. 'No, I mean don't try to be anything. Just relax. This is an awkward time for you and I ought to remember.'

'You've been reading that book again,' I said to tease him.

He flushed. 'Well, I can't know it all. I've got to get it from somewhere.'

In courtship, when we were two single people with no worries and enough money, he had often been top dog. I had seen him as masterful and glamorous; if I had not there would have been no attraction. Now the change was almost complete: a whole repertoire of softer feelings and only fingertip pressure from me to manoeuvre them. It was degrading to have so much power without involvement. I drank my tea.

'Well, anyway,' he went on, 'I'll try to remember.'

'We'll both try,' I said.

He was pleased. 'That's right. Look, I'm sure we'll make out. This last bit may be tough, but when that's over and the baby's here and you're thin again, you'll feel better. And when we get a house we won't be so hard up and – oh, if you really want to keep the car maybe I can get a job in the evenings or at weekends for a while, just to get a bit extra. Or there might be something you'd like to do while I stay at home with the baby. If you weren't studying, that is.'

All this was so pathetic and unnecessary that I was almost tempted to tell him, but of course I didn't. I thought all the same it was time the discussion was closed. 'We'll see,' I said, yawning. 'Let's go to bed now. I'm tired.' I took off my dress and my socks while Malcolm turned out the fire and the lights. As we walked to the bedroom he put an arm round me. Once we were in bed he wanted, very gently and hesitantly, to love me a bit, so I let him.

THIRTY-ONE

MY decision acted on me like a drug. I was more contented than I had ever been since our affair began. Malcolm would have to divorce me eventually, I thought. He would make a very considerate husband for someone who loved him. I still did not quite like to name his feelings for me but I knew they were much too strong and had been developing all the time.

Because I was at peace I assumed the whole world must be too. I pleased my mother and baffled Mrs Ross by my sudden serenity. I let Jean babble away about the baby. There was a wonderful sensation of release: I won't be here. You can all say and do what you like. My being in this state increased the shock when Marianne telephoned me.

She said 'Val, is that you?' but she sounded so faint and far away that I thought she and David must be somewhere on holiday.

'Yes, where are you?' I said.

'At the flat.' Again the barely audible voice. 'Could you come over?'

It had been snowing all morning and I had watched it, on and off, between reading and getting my lunch. The baby had been kicking a lot and I had a pain that felt like indigestion. 'I'm not very mobile,' I said. 'Can't you come over here?'

There was silence, then a whisper: 'I'm in bed.'

I was alarmed. 'Are you ill?'

She said faintly, 'I've only been sick.' Then very quickly though still almost inaudibly, 'Oh Val, he's gone. He found out and he –' She broke off, as far as I could hear, crying.

'Oh Marianne, *no.*'

The soft, whimpering noise went on, like the sound of a tiny animal in pain. She didn't say any more or ask for anything. I wished I felt physically fit. 'All right,' I said. 'I'll come straight away. The same address?'

The noise went on, but she made no answer, so I assumed that meant yes.

I found the journey tiring because I did not really feel like making any journey. When I reached the flat the door was open, so I let myself in. There was no reply when I called Marianne's name. I walked through into the bedroom and she was lying on the bed, fully dressed, her hair all over the place. Her eyes were red and there was a deeply wet patch on the pillow. But now she was making no sound. She didn't look round when I entered.

'Are you all right?' I said, stupid words when she manifestly wasn't, but we all follow conventions more rigidly than ever in a crisis.

'He's gone,' she said. She was staring up at the ceiling. 'He found out.'

I sat on the edge of the bed. 'How?' I asked.

There was a long pause before she answered. It was as though some vital link was severed and she did not realize till minutes later that a question had been asked. 'I don't know,' she said slowly, then added as if in defence, 'He did tell me. But I don't remember.'

'Oh well,' I said, trying to soothe, 'it doesn't matter how.'

'I think he met someone,' she said. 'A boy. Just casually somewhere.' There was no expression in her voice and even now it was unnaturally quiet. She lay there without moving at all.

'I'm so sorry,' I said.

Silence, of course, then, 'It shouldn't have happened.'

I didn't know if she meant it was statistically unlikely or morally wrong, but I said, 'No.'

'I thought . . .' she began, and I leaned forward. But the sentence petered out. I felt very sorry for her but physically and emotionally I was in the wrong gear. It was rather like the opposite of being drunk for an important occasion. I was too sober.

Aware of my shortcomings, I said, 'Would you like some coffee?' and waited for an answer.

Eventually Marianne said, 'I was sick.'

I shivered. It suddenly occurred to me I would have to treat her as a child. The streaming red hair and the smudged mascara were only a mask. Emotionally she had regressed ten years.

'What made you sick?' I asked gently.

Presently she said, 'That was afterwards.' She began to cry again, whimpering between sentences. 'He called me a tramp.' She screwed up her face as if trying to remember. I had seen her look like that at school. 'And a slut. And . . . everything. You know.' A glance in my direction. For the first time she seemed aware of me. I wondered if instead of sitting there trying to stir enough of my numbed feelings to show sympathy, I should really be administering treatment for shock. I compromised, picking the quilt up from the floor and putting it over her.

'He said . . .' she went on, but her face suddenly crumpled up and the tears poured out with fantastic force. I was overwhelmed. I took her hand, but it was cold and limp, neither holding mine nor resisting. Through it, though, I could feel her body shake with the violence of her sobs.

I suddenly noticed an aspirin bottle on the chair beside the bed. It was cloudy with powder, but empty. The words 'I was sick' began to mean something. I picked up the bottle and held it in front of her. 'Did you take these?' I asked rather sharply.

After a moment or two she nodded. 'I was sick,' she said again, between sobs, in tones of failure and humiliation resembling more than anything an athlete who has not cleared a crucial jump. She sounded very tired, as if she had tried her best and it had simply not been good enough.

'Just as well,' I said severely. I felt cold. 'Look, Marianne, you must promise me you'll never do such a silly thing again.'

She looked at me but, I felt pretty sure, without really seeing. 'He's gone,' she said, and the tears spilled over again.

All the conventional stuff about being better off without someone like that would clearly be not only useless but insulting here. I said, 'I'm sorry. I wish I could help.'

She looked away and began pulling feathers out of the quilt, reminding me so much of Emily Brontë's Cathy that I felt quite frightened and had to tell myself not to be stupid.

'I love him so much,' she murmured almost absently, like someone stating something trivial.

'I know.'

Her tears were drying up, leaving a blotched face of extreme youth. She looked so vulnerable that I could have cried myself. The only refuge was cynicism : her problem was she had been too much in love, while I had not been in love at all. Two extremists, suitably rewarded. O wise Sally, with your unwavering code, your moderate feelings, your engagement ring, your bank account.

'Shall I make you some coffee?' I said to Marianne.

'He thinks it makes a difference, finding out,' she said.

'He's jealous,' I attempted. 'He'll probably get over it.'

She looked at me, amazed. 'But I've never loved anyone else.'

I gave her a cigarette and went into the kitchen. I put on the kettle and waited beside it, feeling I could not immediately return to Marianne. It was insoluble. In a sense we were both trying to prove the same point : that our feelings counted for more than our actions. It did not seem a view very popular with anyone else.

When I took the coffee in to her she had pushed away the quilt and was sitting hunched up with her arms round her knees. I held out the cup and she said politely, 'Thank you very much,' like a child at a party, but made no move to take it, so I put it on the chair by the bed and drank my own.

'Maybe he's right,' Marianne said slowly. She looked very thoughtful.

'You know he isn't,' I said.

She shook her head. 'He thinks I'm dirty,' she said.

I was unbearably moved. 'Oh love, don't.' Her tears had dried up completely and there was an alarming control about her. 'Look,' I said, 'why don't you come back with me? Come and stay with us.'

There was a prolonged silence while she stared ahead, still hopelessly far away from me. Then she suddenly turned her head and actually managed a smile. She said in nearly her normal voice, 'Oh Val, that's sweet of you,' as if I had just made the offer that minute.

'All right, that's settled,' I said.

She looked at me kindly. 'No, I can't.'

'Why ever not? Look, if you're worried about David coming back you can leave a note. I'm not trying to get you away from him.'

'He's gone,' she said, in the same calm tone that frightened me.

'Please come,' I said urgently.

Marianne reached out a hand and picked up her coffee cup. She drank and said, 'It's lovely. Thank you.'

'Will you come?'

She shook her head, smiling slightly as if to pacify me.

'Why not? Please, Marianne, I'll be so worried.'

'Don't worry.' She reached for a mirror. 'Oh dear,' she said without expression, 'don't I look a mess.'

'All right,' I said, 'I'll just have to stay here.'

'You can't,' she said, sweetly reasonable. 'Malcolm'll worry about you.'

'I shall phone and explain.'

'There's no need,' she said. 'I'm all right now.'

143

'But I don't want to leave you,' I insisted.

'I'll be better alone.'

I didn't know what to do. 'Look,' I said, 'you phone me tomorrow first thing. All right? If I don't hear by ten I'll phone you. Promise.'

'All right,' she said gently. She touched my arm. 'You've been very good.'

'I haven't,' I said. 'That's just it. I haven't done anything and the little I can do you won't let me.'

'I'm sorry.'

'No, I don't mean that. I don't want you to be sorry. I just want to help.'

'You can't,' she said. 'Nobody can.' She gave me a wide, guileless smile and spoke in the unemotional tones of someone announcing the annual rainfall or the football results. Facts not feelings. It was so unlike her that I was more alarmed than ever. 'How are you feeling?' she went on.

'All right.' Even in more propitious circumstances I would not have told her or anyone my new intentions.

'That's good,' she said. From regressing to childhood she now seemed years older than I was, which made me doubly unable to cope with her. I hung on a little longer, but there was nothing to be said and I felt in the way. 'Well, if you're sure,' I said eventually, 'I'll go. But remember, you've got to ring me before ten tomorrow.'

She saw me to the door but we didn't embrace as usual. 'You *have* been good,' she said.

I panicked again. 'Please change your mind and come,' I said.

She shook her head. 'I'll be better alone.'

So I left her.

I stood in the bus queue amongst the homegoing crowds and worried. I hardly noticed the cold. The morning snow was already brown and slushy with foot- and tyre-marks. When I got home I told Malcolm briefly what had happened, but he thought she was probably expecting David back that night

144

and wanted to be alone and waiting for him. 'It wouldn't be the same if she came here,' he said.

I was not convinced, but I didn't like to phone in case she thought it was David, or later in case Malcolm was right and I interrupted a reconciliation. I slept badly, though, and was awake in good time and waiting for the phone. Time crawled slowly in the flat and the silence was almost palpable. I was anxious and nervous. At twenty to ten, though, telling myself I would probably only rouse her from sleep badly needed, I dialled Marianne's number. There was no reply. I let it ring for a while, then gave up. Shopping, I decided. The more unreachable a person is, the more you are forced to invent a life for them to excuse their behaviour or allay your fears. I tried again at very frequent intervals. Had Malcolm been right? Had David come back and they both disappeared? Or what?

All day I tried, till I entirely lost count. But the phone rang and rang.

THIRTY-TWO

THAT evening I couldn't rest until Malcolm had driven me over to Marianne's flat. There was no reply to the doorbell and we were hesitating on the step wondering if we would be justified in breaking down the door, when a woman came out of another flat and informed us that Marianne had left early that morning with suitcases. Alone, she added, when we inquired. We apologized for disturbing her, as she was in a dressing-gown, and left.

'D'you suppose they're all kept women in that block of flats?' Malcolm asked.

'I've no idea,' I said shortly. 'I don't think Marianne is any more.'

'Well, at least we know she hasn't done anything silly,' Malcolm said.

'Do we?'

'Well, that woman saw her go out.'

'That doesn't tell us what happened after that or where she is now.'

'Oh Val, don't be so gloomy. She may be back with David, right this minute.'

'Or under a bus.' I couldn't understand why she hadn't phoned me.

I might have continued indefinitely in this state, with Malcolm's optimism driving me mad, but two days later I got a postcard in Marianne's childish handwriting saying, 'Am all right. Don't worry. Love. M.' No address, though, or phone number. Posted in town. Once again she had gone to earth.

Relieved, I gave more time and effort to the relaxation and breathing exercises I had been taught. Now that I knew that I was leaving soon after, I could face the birth more readily. I wanted it to go well, partly so that I would soon be fit enough to go, but also because it was a challenge to me physically, much as a tennis match or a swimming gala would have been. I wanted to perform well and not let myself down.

My apparent enthusiasm and new cheerfulness pleased Malcolm, who was putting all his energy into decorating and preparing the nursery. I agreed with all his suggestions, since I would not have to live with them, and this made him happy. Once or twice Jeff and his new girl-friend Carol called in, or other members of the crowd Malcolm used to go around with. He never went out with any of them now because he couldn't afford to buy them drinks. They were still smoking, of course, which didn't help either. I wished he would go out sometimes; in fact I wished he wasn't so obviously determined to become a model husband when I was so far from being a model wife. I suggested robbing the post office, but he was shocked. The money in there appeared to be sacred. I hoped he would get good and drunk on it after my departure, but it didn't seem very likely. He had changed a lot.

He still read his book on pregnancy and childbirth, glancing up occasionally as he discovered a new fact about me, sometimes asking about symptoms I hadn't had and others I hadn't mentioned.

'But I didn't know. Why didn't you say you felt like that?'

'It was easier not to think about it,' I explained patiently, 'let alone talk about it. The more you admit it, the worse it gets.'

He looked puzzled, disappointed. 'I should've thought it was the other way round.'

'Well, it isn't. Not for me. Anyway, I haven't been too bad really.'

'Haven't you?' He brightened. 'That's good.' And returned to the book. The book and the nursery began to rule our lives. He was either in there, pottering around, or sitting opposite me reading all about the great event.

Alone during the day I was restless, now, too excited to work. In less than a month it would be over. In a few weeks after that, I could go. I was like a child looking forward to the circus. When I looked in the mirror my face was pale with anticipation. I moved round a lot, doing nothing in particular. At night it was hard to sleep. If I could have done so safely I would have used a calendar and marked off the days. Oh God, I thought, to be slim again and have normal breasts and feel like a human being.

I tried to plan soberly what to tell my mother. I would write her a letter, not exposing the whole truth, of course, but saying that my feelings for Malcolm had faded as his for me had increased, and that I had no interest in the baby. For these reasons I thought it best to leave and hoped she would understand. I could not imagine what she could say to Jean. I knew really that I ought to write Jean a letter, too, but that was even harder. Yet, although this hurt and worried me, it was not the same as the desperation I had felt before the wedding. A few months' experience had changed me, perhaps even more mentally than physically. I had to save myself. No one else would.

I looked at my mother, when she came to see me and give me pep-talks about the baby, and thought in a numb way, as I heard and answered her remarks, what a dreadful thing I was going to do to her. I tried to picture her reaction. She was so wise and tolerant: there must be a good chance that she could accept my behaviour. I was revealing as little as I could; it would not be complete disillusion. Perhaps she could find some way of explaining to Jean without hurting her or making her hate me. It was bad luck that Jean was so fond of Malcolm and so much more maternal than I was. But there was really no alternative. If I stayed I would only break down in front of her and Mother. I would loathe the baby and make Malcolm wretched.

I couldn't find a solution for Jean but I hoped that my mind might function better once I was no longer pregnant. Safely in London, at a distance, I could write letters of explanation. I planned to stay at a hostel and get a job, any job and study at night until I could get another university place. I didn't care how long it might take. I knew now that I could live on very little.

Our budget in fact seemed tighter than ever. It was so precisely balanced that even the fact of my not feeling equal to walking till I found the lowest prices made a difference. So much money seemed to go in gas and electricity that in the worst of the weather I stayed in bed late and we tried to go to bed early. I got tired of scraping without the compensation of knowing that it was all worthwhile. Occasionally I had glimpses of what it might have been like if I had been in love with Malcolm and happy about the baby, and the contrast was shattering: like a black and white film going suddenly into technicolour.

In March my life seemed to be at a standstill. Mrs Franklin returned my last essay with a letter saying she was going to France at Easter, so could do no more till next term and perhaps I would be too busy by then to write essays. It occurred to me that for all the talk at school about education really mattering and exams not being all-important, she was not very interested in my work now that it had no apparent aim. Then I remembered how we had discussed her at school, whether she was over thirty, when if ever she would start a family. For the first time it struck me, a piece of superb irony, that she might actually envy me. Perhaps she would like to look after the baby. Maybe I should give it to her. I thought actually that Malcolm's mother would most likely be landed with it and it would serve her right for the things she had said to me. No doubt she would love it, though; so much the better, really. I was not out for revenge, only deliverance.

Through all my self-preoccupations, an awareness of Marianne nagged me like toothache. I had heard nothing. Gradually I was forced to accept that she was well if not happy, since bad news travels so fast. I still vaguely listened for the phone and watched for the post, but I couldn't keep it up. After all, Marianne had disappeared so many times before. I could only wait for her to contact me, if in fact she did so before I left.

I wanted the baby to come early now; I felt unbearably tense and withdrawn. I had waited long enough; I wanted action. My mood reached Malcolm and ours became a very jumpy household. I began dropping plates and he started knocking nails into his thumb. Conversation, such as it was, became riddled with 'Not long now' and similar phrases full of double meaning for me.

Sometimes I looked at him and from my vantage point of near-escape felt nothing but pure pity. He had tried so hard. It was not his fault he was the wrong person. I could only feel this pity now that I was no longer physically involved with him. We still made love, though less often now that it was awkward, and he assumed my remoteness was due to pregnancy alone. He looked forward to a reunion afterwards, he said.

'You have to wait six weeks,' I reminded him. He knew. He had read it in his little book. In fact we would never make love again after the baby arrived, but he couldn't know that. In the short while remaining there were only a few times left, at our now reduced rate. In a way it was a strange thought.

When the snow finally melted we had rain and more rain. Sometimes I went out in it, perversely, and got soaked. It was a kind of outlet for all the ordinary physical things I couldn't do. And I think I also wanted to punish my body for being so repulsive. I actually felt a little more comfortable than I had for some time, although I had resumed my frequent recourse to the lavatory, which I found humiliating, but there was no doubt I looked awful. Enormous, anyway. Sometimes when I looked at myself full-length in the mirror – and full was the key word – I put out my tongue in disgust or said, 'Ridiculous' out loud.

After the rain we had gales. March was going out like a lion. I remembered that as one of the earliest things I had learnt in junior or infant school, when it had seemed like a piece of real scientific information to be treasured. My hair was ragged from a winter of neglect and I felt beyond cutting it myself, so I went to Sally. Knowing the baby could be early or late, I was becoming rather nervous of being caught with my hair as messy as the rest of me.

Sally was solicitous as usual ('How're you feeling?') and predictable ('Not long now!') all of which I put up with. But she seemed excited and wrought up about something, and was no different even when I had religiously asked her all about her forthcoming wedding: clothes, food, guests, honeymoon, house. She started cutting, but there was a funny look on her face. Presently she said, 'Val, d'you ever hear from Marianne these days?'

'Up to a month ago,' I said, to save time and effort.

She went on looking openly secretive and embarrassed and it suddenly struck me I was meant to inquire further. Then I had a suspicion she had somehow heard Marianne was pregnant and didn't know how to tell me. I couldn't imagine why I had not thought of it before. 'What about her?' I said.

Sally concentrated very hard on the hair she was cutting and said, 'Anne Dawson saw her in town the other day.' She paused, then looked straight at my reflection. 'In a doorway. Picking up men.'

I stared back at her. She was clearly shocked, yet she was getting some sort of kick from the situation. Her attitude deflected my concentration from her words, lessening the shock.

I said, 'Are you sure?' and I had not really absorbed the information.

'Anne's sure. And Joan saw something in the paper about her being had up for soliciting.' It came out in a rush now. 'They gave her name.'

I was cold. Why had I never expected this? I said, 'Marianne . . .' as if she were in the room.

Sally said, 'Yes, it said Marianne Hart and her age and something about the Street Offences Act. Isn't it awful?'

I didn't answer and she went on cutting. 'It makes me feel so funny to think I've been to school with someone who's doing that. And we were all so friendly. I thought she was supposed to be so keen on David Whatsit.'

I said, 'Yes. She is. Far more than he deserves.'

'Well, then, how can she do a thing like that?'

I was defeated by the enormity of attempting to explain to Sally. 'He left her,' I said briefly.

'Oh, did he? Oh dear. But still . . .' She stressed the word and let it drift away. 'I don't know how she can. I always knew she was a bit . . . fast but I never thought she'd do a thing like that.'

I jerked my head out of her hands.

'Oh, I hadn't finished,' she said, surprised.

'I can finish it myself,' I said.

She looked at me suspiciously. 'Are you all right? I hope I haven't given you too much of a shock.'

I picked up the scissors and briefly cut the remaining piece of hair. How I looked suddenly seemed very unimportant. I put the money beside a comb.

'I'm fine,' I said. 'I hope you have a lovely wedding.'

THIRTY-THREE

BUT there was nothing I could do. I just kept thinking of Marianne and seeing her face. All the things she had said went round and round in my mind. I didn't tell Malcolm about Sally's information. When he said, 'Oh, you've had your hair cut,' I just said, 'Yes,' and when he said, 'It's nice,' I replied, 'Thank you.' Knowing how Marianne loved David only proved that to behave like that she must have nothing to live for. Then I remembered how she had said, 'Perhaps he's right', and 'He thinks I'm dirty', and I began to see a terrifying logic. If David the god was wrong she could make him right by sinking to the level he had prescribed for her.

In bed I lay awake when I thought Malcolm was asleep, but I must have been more restless than I realized because he suddenly said in a perfectly wide-awake voice, 'Val, are you all right?'

I said, 'Fine.'

'You haven't got a pain?'

I started to say no, but he made me consider how I felt. In fact I did have a very slight pain which I had not noticed before, being too busy thinking. Foolishly, caught off balance, I said 'Only a tiny one.'

'My God, you've started.' In an instant he sat up in bed and switched on the light. 'How far apart are they?'

I was startled and cross. 'What?' I said, as forcefully as I could.

'The contractions.' His hair was on end and he looked frantic.

I had to laugh at the professional jargon. 'They are not contractions,' I said. 'I had a small pain and it's gone.'

Immediately he looked at his watch. 'Tell me when you get another one.'

I couldn't believe we were to spend the night like this. 'Malcolm, I'm not going to get another one.'

He ignored me. 'When they're twenty minutes apart I'm going to take you to hospital. That's right, isn't it? Don't worry; you'll be okay.'

'I'm okay now,' I said, although the more he went on the less sure I was. We waited in tense silence until I felt quite hysterical. 'You're going to be awfully tired in the morning,' I said.

'What does that matter?' He seemed surprised. 'Can I get you anything? A drink? A hot-water bottle?'

'Oh no,' I said. 'Good heavens no. I'm perfectly all right.'

'You must tell me when you have another pain.'

'I'd much rather go to sleep,' I said.

'But you can't if this is it.'

'I don't think it is. It's too early.'

'But it could be early.'

'Yes, it could.' I felt exhausted by his energy.

'Don't you really think it is?'

'No,' I said. 'I don't.'

'But how can you tell?'

'Oh, I don't know,' I said wearily. 'It's too early and it doesn't feel right.'

'But you've never felt it before.' He sounded almost indignant.

'And you?' I inquired.

He was silent, thinking. 'I suppose it could be a false labour,' he said eventually.

'Oh, doubtless,' I said.

'Well, it can happen. I should have thought before.'

'It's in your book, is it?'

He looked at me closely. 'I'm sorry. How else can I find out?'

'You could go to fatherhood classes,' I said, joking.

'I didn't like to.' He sounded serious, even ashamed. 'I wish I had now.'

'Oh God.' I turned over.

'What's the matter?' He leaned over me. 'Another pain?'

'No,' I said.

All the same, we had a wretched night. About half an hour later, as if a judgement on me, I did have another pain and began to wonder if Malcolm was going to be proved right after all. He got excited again and we spent ages waiting for the next one. But they gradually got weaker and further apart until we had wasted hours over them. In spite of myself I felt, though tried not to convey, a sense of anticlimax.

'I think it's all over,' I said finally. 'If you start now you can just about get three hours' sleep.'

'It doesn't matter,' he said. 'I don't feel tired.'

'You will in the morning.'

'Yes, I suppose so.'

He cleared teacups from the bedroom and put out the light. We lay on our backs, exhausted but wide awake.

'Don't think I can sleep,' he said.

I was thinking how everything had changed: how much more solemn he was, how I had become remote, how Marianne's life was smashed. A year ago, how much happier we had all been. And now this ordeal lay ahead, had nearly come, and that would be the end. I would have to start again, start properly. I felt very unreal, very five o'clock in the morning.

'Val,' Malcolm said, 'it makes you think, doesn't it, a false alarm like that?'

I didn't answer at first. My brain moved slowly but with great power like a car in first gear: how pointless was the boring life I led. The incredible monotony of bed, night after night, that I had once been so glad to jump into. The incessant routine of shopping and cleaning, cooking and washing up. Sending Malcolm to the laundrette in the car. Day following day with nothing to distinguish any of them.

'Think what?' I asked.

'Oh, I don't know.' He hesitated. 'How ... sort of casual we were, to start with. You know, way back. And now here we are. I mean, this is what it's really all about.'

He never made jokes any more. He had gone all reverent and mystical. I should have to write him a letter, too, when I left. All those letters. I sighed.

'Well, you know,' he went on. 'This is really something and it's happening to us. I mean, it's important.'

I didn't answer. He said urgently, 'Val, can I be there?'

'Where?'

'With you. In hospital, when it's born. I never thought about it before. But just now – well, I think I'd go off my head if I had to wait somewhere. I want to be with you. There must be something I can do – hold your hand, rub your back. I want to help. I won't look at anything if you don't want me to. I just want to be with you.'

I was very taken aback but forced myself to think quickly. 'They don't like it in hospitals,' I said. 'There aren't many where you can do that.'

'Maybe this is one. We could ask. I'll ring them up tomorrow.'

'No.' My voice was sharp and I tried to modulate it when I spoke again. 'I'd rather you didn't. I ... don't really want you to be there.'

There was a painful silence, then he said in a lost-sounding voice, 'Don't you?'

'I'm sorry,' I said. 'I think I'll ... behave better and get on faster by myself. It would put me off to have anyone there who didn't have to be.'

'Then I can't come?'

I felt he was being childish and I was annoyed yet pitying at the same time. 'I'd rather you didn't,' I said.

Another pause. 'Oh Val, I'll be so worried.'

'Well then,' I said, justified. 'That wouldn't help me, would it?'

'No, I mean just waiting. I'd be all right if I was with you.'

'Well, I wouldn't,' I said finally.

'But I don't want you to go through all this by yourself. After all, I got you into it.'

'God,' I shouted suddenly. 'Are you starting all that again?'

'All what?'

'Taking sole responsibility. Being so bloody generous.'

'I'm sorry,' he said, sounding puzzled. 'But you know what I mean. I'd like us to see it through together.'

I had to try another approach, and quickly. 'That's just it,' I said. 'You'd distract me. I'd be worried how you were feeling. I'd never keep my mind on my work.'

He said slowly, 'Would you really feel like that?'

I didn't answer but cast round for further aid. 'I might make awful noises and upset you and really it might only be effort. So I'd end up trying to be quiet and that might make it worse. Don't you see? I wouldn't feel free to be natural.' I stopped and gasped at my own duplicity.

'All right,' he said at last. 'If that's how you feel. But you'd better be quick, that's all. Before I go round the bend.'

Next day to my amazement he brought me flowers and brushed aside my thanks. Memory of the night's events seemed to embarrass him. I felt embarrassed, too, hemmed in by affection and concern. My mother and Jean came to see me, and Malcolm's parents, though I had never been alone with his mother since our big scene. It was unpleasant to be the focus of everyone's attention. I felt like a zoo exhibit that had been coaxed into breeding in captivity. The suspense in the atmosphere tortured me: everything was ready and at a standstill. I lumbered around on swollen ankles and Malcolm leaped up to fetch things and urged me to rest. The date came and went and I felt foolish to be found still in the flat when Malcolm came home at night. Knowing first babies were often late was no help; I still felt like a guest without the sense to tell when a party was over. So it was nothing but pure relief one afternoon three days later to feel unmistakable and blissfully clockwork pains reinforced by blood. I was all alone and I felt quite religious in my gratitude. I wanted no one. I didn't care what lay ahead. The sooner it happened, the sooner I would be free and everything would be over. I felt very excited and capable and tough. But the presence of anyone, even my mother being a tower of strength, would have enraged me. I wanted to yell with sudden energy. Instead I collected my things together and phoned for a taxi. I knew I should make other telephone calls or at least leave a note, but I didn't want to, so I didn't. I took perverse delight in doing what I knew was the wrong thing : departing without a word. This, above all, was surely a time to please myself. So I told no one, and when the taxi came I was ready for it. I even enjoyed spending money I couldn't afford. It never occurred to me to call an ambulance. I would have bought champagne if there had been time.

PART 3

THIRTY-FOUR

IRONICALLY enough, I approached the whole thing in what was a text-book frame of mind. I was calm and trained. I had always had my body under good control and there was no reason why it should let me down now. I would have been ashamed to be frightened, and besides, to show fear would have put me in the power of others. When Malcolm asked me afterwards if I had had a bad time I said quite honestly, 'I don't know.' I was in the position of a man who had seen only one egg. How could he be expected to know if it was small, medium or large?

A girl near me screamed and screamed till I asked if she was in great pain. It turned out that she found it a help to scream. Some effort was made to stop her but without much success. It seemed all very well for her, but I wished she had tried to imagine what the hospital would have been like if everyone had yelled continually. All my community feelings, not exercised since school, returned. There was almost a teacher's pet atmosphere: those who behaved well were popular with the staff.

I felt very self-important, having finally reached this point. When the pain got bad I tried to comfort myself by reflecting how much worse it would have been if Malcolm had been there to sympathize and worry. I could understand why some women wanted to crawl into a bush to have their babies – or was that elephants going away to die? There wasn't much difference, anyway. I didn't think about the baby as such, but about whether I was relaxing, breathing, *surviving* properly. It worried me a little that I had no way of knowing how much worse it was going to get or how long it would last. Average figures or vague generalizations no longer comfort when it is your turn. Not knowing meant I couldn't ration out my strength exactly. When Malcolm saw me he said, 'You look tired,' in an odd voice, and I actually laughed. He flushed and apologized for making a stupid remark, but as if it had meant something else. I tried to think how I really felt: tired, sore, stretched, aching, and decided the word that came nearest was 'mangled'. All that pushing and shoving and sweating so that they could finally drag out a thing like a skinned rabbit with a huge and apparently deformed head. I didn't care. I wouldn't be around to see it grow up, but everyone assured me it was perfectly normal. A lovely little girl, they said, and it made weird noises. They showed it to me and I looked down at my acres of flat stomach, the deflated balloon. Towards the end I had pushed, inspired not so much by 'I will be free' as by 'I will be thin'. Then I did look at the child and it definitely seemed sub-human, a strange colour, and hairy. All the same, I felt odd: I had produced that, I had a daughter. It was absurd.

I wanted terribly to sleep but when I did I dreamed I was pregnant again. Not fat, actually, at all, but certainly pregnant and it was all going to last much longer this time. People in the dream turned into other people before I had time to identify them, but they all seemed to take it for granted that I would be pregnant for years. I woke up sweating. The girl who had screamed was sleeping peacefully; she had finished long before me though we had begun more or less together. There was no justice.

'Was it awful?' Malcolm asked again on his next visit, looking guilty.

'I had some stuff to help,' I said, not knowing really what to tell him. Then the look on his face annoyed me suddenly and I said as if it were a casual thought, 'The worst part was when I thought I was going to split in two.'

He flinched dreadfully and I was immediately better and ashamed of myself at the same time. He didn't answer, though, and I didn't know what to say next.

They were annoyed with me in hospital because I wouldn't feed the baby. I could have asked Malcolm to get tough with them, although he didn't like what I was doing, but I preferred to handle it myself. I don't think anyone could have overcome the prejudice, though; I always seemed last to be given a bottle when breasts were bared, and the baby was left with me, screaming. But others, unable to breast-feed and virtuously desolated by their inability, were waited on promptly. In the end I complained very clearly to a doctor, and the service speeded up somewhat. I wasn't popular, though. I suppose to them I was being unnatural (the worst of all crimes and something different to every person) and I was also making extra work. An odd retaliation, though, from people professing to care about the child's welfare: she certainly suffered more from it than I did, and I thought as I looked at her turning mauve with frustration how unfair it was that she should go hungry just because I didn't want to feed her. It would have been more logical to deprive me of food.

The food was institutional and reminded me of school. In fact the whole place was rather like a boarding-school, only the staff not the pupils were in uniform. There was even a small hierachy of prefects: Caesarians and mothers of twins. There was a school-like awareness of time and a certain amount of regimentation; necessary, I suppose. This didn't bother me, but I could have done without the communal washrooms. So many partly clothed women, none in their best shape, and some positively huge from multiple child-bearing – a depressing sight.

Malcolm thought the baby was lovely. He looked so shy when he said it that you'd have thought it was an effort, yet he managed to say it every time he came. I got sick of hearing it. He kept on at me about names, too. His parents thought

Elizabeth was a beautiful name and would go well with Ross, but remembering Christmas I thought they were probably being patriotic. I had nothing against the name Elizabeth, that is until I heard they liked it. Malcolm favoured Elaine. He brought it out very hesitantly ('I thought maybe Elaine') and waited. I said, 'Oh, I don't know. Can't we leave it a bit?' My mother, of course, expressed no preferences. Fresh alternatives came from his parents: Helen, Jennifer, Margaret, Pauline. He sat at my bedside with a book of names and thumbed through it. Everyone else seemed to have names ready and the Johns and Davids multiplied around us. I had intended to agree to anything, since I felt it impertinent to choose a name for a child that would never answer to it in my presence, but with every name that was suggested I became more hostile. I wanted an announcement in the papers, though, because I was sure that would make Marianne contact me, and no doubt it would look better if it contained a name, to say nothing of the registration or birth certificate Malcolm keep mentioning. One way and another it seemed a name was becoming vital. Logically, of course, I should have let Mrs Ross have her way since she was in for the surprise of bringing the baby up, but I became stubborn. After all, I had put a lot of effort, however unwillingly, into producing the baby and it now seemed that I deserved to choose a name. I made my mind a blank in which, as I waited for inspiration, the name Vicky suddenly appeared.

'Vicky,' I said to Malcolm who was, as it happened, for once talking about something else.

'What? Oh.' He was startled. 'Victoria, d'you mean?' He tried it over. 'Victoria Ross. It's a bit of a mouthful.'

'No,' I said. 'Just Vicky.'

'Oh.' He hesitated. 'Any special reason?'

'My father was called Vic,' I said. But I had only just remembered this. I knew it would clinch any argument, such is the power of the dead and near in blood, but in fact I liked the name because it had come to me when I needed it and no one else had thought of it and it sounded tough. She would have to be tough.

'Fine,' said Malcolm. 'Vicky Ross. That sounds good.' And I felt a surge of power at having imposed a name on the child. Wherever I was, she would bear that mark of me.

Whenever I handled the baby, and I got plenty of practice in hospital, I felt a sense of inexpressible strangeness that I was her mother, or for that matter anyone's mother, I, Valerie Ayden – Ross – aged twenty. The physical reality of the baby increased this sensation; doing mundane tasks such as feeding and changing her, which I soon learnt and the difficulty of which I thought must be exaggerated by most people for comic effect, made it all the more fantastic that she was my daughter. I could not explain this properly even to myself but I felt it very strongly. The nine months had dragged, certainly, yet now I seemed to be quite suddenly in charge of this new creature who seemed almost to have come from nowhere. How could she be the lump I had carried inside me, that had made me sore and kicked me and kept me awake? Having spent so long preparing for this precise eventuality, I found it took me by surprise. I said something like this to my mother and she appeared to find it normal and understandable, but she confused it with mother love, so I gave up trying to explain how I felt. It was too difficult in any case. In its simplest terms it was that I found the whole event quite unbelievable.

Back in the flat I was besieged with visitors. Jean, of course, worshipped the baby and was in the first flush of ecstatic aunthood, taking full advantage of the Easter holidays to practically live with us until my mother gently suggested she should call less often. This emerged from a long and devious conversation in which, it turned out later, Jean was trying to find out if she was, as my mother thought, wearing me out. She was so cunning in her inquiry that I had no idea what we were talking about and she ended in tears because she believed I was pretending not to understand, not wishing to tell her that Mother was right. When she sobbed all this out I hugged her and promised to tell Mother very casually but as soon as possible how useful she was. I would have said this anyway, for Jean in tears always demoralized me and I was glad she cried seldom, but it was in fact true. With her in the flat I was free to go shopping quickly without the pram, or cook without interruption, and she was always keen to take Vicky out for a walk. I agreed because it gave Jean pleasure but I could see no more point in it than I had ever seen. The baby could not take exercise and she could breathe no more air in motion than she could while static in the garden. But to Jean it was something you did and she walked herself virtually to collapse, convinced that she was doing Vicky boundless good. 'Seeing Jean with Vicky,' said my mother, 'makes me wish I could have had more children. All these years Jean must have wanted a younger sister.'

During these outings I relaxed. At first I tried to work but I had no power to concentrate. I decided it might be more realistic to wait until I was in London – say in about a month. I wanted to be really fit and back to normal first; I was disappointed on leaving hospital to find how easily I tired. People assured me that everyone was like this, which made it even more depressing. So when Jean took Vicky out I sat with my feet up, ate vitamins and played cheerful music on the gramophone. I thought at first that I should be more energetic, but even the simple exercises I had to do for muscle- and figure-improvement exhausted me. 'You mustn't do too much,' Malcolm kept saying. He started coming back from work pretending he felt like cooking supper when I knew he must be tired. Still, I was tired too, so I let him. He kept turning up, though, in the nursery and the bathroom to see what I was doing. 'You're awfully efficient,' he said, almost wistfully.

'It's not difficult,' I said. 'They show you what to do and you do it.' Vicky, of course, chose that moment to squirm and I speared my thumb. Malcolm registered the pain and laughed at the same time.

'Don't be too cocky,' he said.

To my amazement I said, 'Damn you,' and burst into tears. I abandoned Vicky, half in and half out of her nappy, and rushed into the bedroom, sobbing wildly. I had no self-control at all. It was months since I had cried and it seemed to be an enormous, horrible flood. I hadn't even known I wanted to cry; I hadn't known I was miserable. My behaviour took me entirely by surprise and the remnant of myself that stood by and watched was totally astounded and quite powerless to intervene. After a while (I was still howling, screaming almost) Malcolm came into the bedroom and put a hand on my shoulder.

'Go away,' I yelled at him. I hated him, I hated Vicky, I hated myself. I was consumed with hatred for the whole world.

He stood beside me irresolutely, then said, 'It's quite natural.'

'Get out,' I shrieked. I hated everyone and everything, but most of all I hated being told how normal I was.

THIRTY-FIVE

OF course I got over this. It disgusted me, so I told myself toughly that it was ludicrous to crack up now, so near deliverance. But it is usually the last part of any ordeal that is the hardest to bear.

The baby's appearance improved, not that there was much else it could do. I was pleased – illogically, since it would not affect me and so should not matter – because it seemed a point of honour to hand her over in good condition and looking presentable, like washing a dress before you give it away. To the family, however, she had been delightful from the start, and they all (even my mother, I was disappointed to note) spent hours tracing imaginary resemblances. Mrs Ross in particular hung over the cot or pram till I longed to push her into it. She was convinced the baby looked like Malcolm. To my mother she was the image of Jean at the same age. No one suggested she might be like me. To my mind it was ridiculous trying to discover any likeness so early, especially as Malcolm and I were both dark, with regular features.

Malcolm's mother was now a frequent visitor, full of praise for the baby and the way I managed. 'She's a real credit to you,' she said more than once. It was as if she was begging me to forget we had ever insulted each other, and I suppose her seeing a resemblance to Malcolm was in itself a form of apology. She was dreadfully thorough, asking me detailed questions about Vicky's progress that I could hardly answer but nevertheless always appearing satisfied with the answers. She shoved her large face in front of Vicky and made a re-

petitive, monotonous sound that might be rendered phoneti-
cally as *Watchicoo*. I listened to this with amazement and
disgust, delighted occasionally when Vicky responded with a
howl of alarm. Sometimes this turned against me. Mrs Ross
might pick her up with an eager 'Come to Granny then', but
she might also thrust her at me, declaring, 'Ah, she wants
her mummy, don't you, pet?' I was then supposed to sit and
cuddle her and behave like an idiot while Grandmother
beamed adoringly. I hated people to watch me with Vicky
if I knew she required neither feeding nor changing nor attention to wind, so I usually responded to this by saying firmly,
'She wants a rest; she's tired,' replacing Vicky in the pram
or cot and shutting the door. Mrs Ross and I then sat out or
pretended not hear the screams. Sometimes she would say
with a mournful expression, 'Yes, you do have to be firm with
them,' and finally, with more approval, when Vicky's protests
ceased, 'Ah, she knows who's boss all right.'

I missed Jean badly when she returned to school. With all
my determination I found it as much as I could do to keep
pace with the housework, shopping and cooking. Vicky in-
truded on my routine, such as it was. I never seemed able
to start and finish a job without having to stop to do something for her. By the end of the day I was exhausted and longing to sink into bed. I fell asleep instantly while Malcolm was
still turning over. The night feed was a chore but when I complained about it Malcolm said, 'It'd be easier if you were
feeding her yourself.'

'She's all right,' I said sharply. Two o'clock is not a good
hour to thrash out fundamentals.

'Okay,' he said. 'I only meant it would be easier for you.'

I turned my back and sulked and listened to his breathing,
which sounded very much awake. He was, I supposed, fru-
trated. He had already said a few times how nice it would
be when the six weeks were up. He had not touched me at
all since I came back from hospital, even by way of a casual

caress. I felt he was afraid of my body after all it had been through, and I was glad. To my relief I felt no return of desire. I was free. I realized now, fully, how sex could imprison and subjugate you. My physical dependence on Malcolm had given him power and put me, however spasmodically, at his mercy. I might as well have been at the end of a long chain which he could tug when he felt inclined. Now it was broken; or it was he who was tied to the end of it.

I became so used to expecting that he would not touch me that one night I was almost shocked when he reached out a hand.

'You know I can't,' I said promptly, blessing medical science and wishing it could extend my immunity in case I didn't manage to escape punctually next month.

There was a long pause, then he said with difficulty, 'Play Solitaire?' which was an old joke of ours.

I had known really that this was inevitable but I waited a while before responding. I didn't want even this much reminder of our former life. Then I took pity on him and reached out my hand. But when he tried to touch me I moved away.

'Aren't you playing?' he asked in a plaintive voice.

'No,' I said, 'I'm not playing.' I waited for him to be offended and prepared my defence, but he made no reply and so the performance continued. His rapture seemed indecent because it was displayed to someone who felt no involvement; I was sure he could have no idea how detached I was. I had to remind myself how important this had once been to me, and then I felt only pity for him because he was not free of it as I was. My mind roamed away on books, shopping, a visit to my mother on her half day; my skill was automatic and I was only drawn back to the present by a voice moaning my name. Then it was all over and I couldn't avoid him embracing me and kissing me in a sort of frantic, humble way. 'Oh Val,' he kept saying, and, 'it's been so long.' Eventually he let me go and lit a rare cigarette while I tried to get comfortable in the hot and sticky bed.

'I'll make it up to you,' he said presently. 'When you're feeling fit again, we'll have a great time. It'll be worth waiting for.'

I kissed him to avoid answering.

THIRTY-SIX

Just when I had given up all hope of hearing from Marianne and had almost, having so many distractions, stopped worrying about her, she appeared on my doorstep. No phone call, no postcard: she was suddenly there. She looked nervous, unsure of her welcome, but otherwise unchanged: maybe paler and thinner but still attractive in a new blue suit and high heels, with her hair as profuse as ever. She surprised me, so I must have been, idiotically, expecting God knows what marks of shame and degradation.

'Hullo, Val,' she said. 'Can I come in?'

I got over my surprise and flung my arms round her, but she only squeezed me gently, nothing like the old desperate hug.

'I should've come sooner,' she said.

I laughed. 'We're only just on speaking terms,' I said. 'Oh well, never mind. You're here now.'

She followed me upstairs saying, 'I was afraid you'd moved.'

'Why didn't you phone?'

She made no reply. Instead she said eagerly, 'Can I see the baby?'

'Oh,' I said. 'Is that all you've come for? You don't care how I am . . .'

She stood still on the landing and stared at me. 'You look marvellous,' she said. Then I caught her gaze wandering to the nursery door.

'All right,' I said. 'Come on.'

Vicky was asleep. Marianne crept in as though the merest sound would wake her and stood reverently at the bottom of the cot. I watched her face; after all, I could look at Vicky any time. The expression of envy and tenderness on Marianne's face made me feel an intruder.

'Oh,' she breathed. 'Isn't she lovely?'

It did not sicken me as it had from others. In a way it seemed only a transference of the love Marianne had always displayed when she talked of David. She had always had so much more love to give than I had, and with less encouragement. Looking at her, I found myself thinking that Vicky should be her baby.

Marianne smiled and I thought that if David could see her now he would surely implore her forgiveness – or shoot himself for being such a fool. 'Her little hands,' said Marianne in a whisper.

To someone else I would have said briskly, 'Yes, it's amazing how often I have to cut her nails,' or something similar to check emotion, but to Marianne I said only, 'Yes, they're sweet.'

'Oh Val,' Marianne said after a long pause. 'She's beautiful.' Her eyelids were fluttering and I realized with alarm that she was going to cry. While I was still wondering what to do, she seemed to recover herself, smiled at me and tiptoed out of the nursery. I followed and shut the door.

'Come and sit down,' I said. 'The kettle was on before you came. It won't take long.'

We went into the living-room. Marianne groped in her bag for cigarettes.

'It's lovely to see you,' I said as we lit up. 'But really I ought to murder you. Remember a certain phone call?'

She looked guilty, yet also vague. 'Oh yes,' she said. 'I never rang, did I?'

'Not only that,' I said. 'You decamped. You took off in the night, practically, and when we came round you'd gone.'

'I'm sorry,' she said, but more as if a misfortune had befallen me than something she could have controlled. She frowned. 'Didn't I write, though?'

'A postcard,' I said pointedly.

'Oh yes.' She smiled at me, still a child under the makeup. I felt older than ever. 'I thought I did.'

'I was very worried,' I said. 'You were in such a state when I left you . . . and to hear nothing . . .'

'Oh, I'm sorry,' she said again, in a low, gentle voice. 'Don't be cross with me. That's why I had to come. I didn't like to ring up.'

She stopped, and I felt bound to abandon such an unprofitable subject. 'Did you see the papers?' I asked.

Her face brightened. 'Oh yes. I bought them all for weeks. I was so excited.' Again the vague look. 'I meant to write.'

'It doesn't matter,' I said, 'I knew you wouldn't really.'

'No,' she said absently. 'I'm hopeless, aren't I?'

I smiled at her. 'Just a hopeless correspondent. Anyway – how are you?' I didn't know how to make her talk; I could hardly weigh in with 'Guess what Sally said about you.' There was no direct approach I could use : you do not look your friend in the eye and say, 'Tell me, is it true you've become a prostitute? If she hasn't, she can be annoyed with you for believing a rumour; if she has, it is hard to find a suitable comment.

'All right,' she said.

'I've been so worried about you,' I said. 'On and off, you know, in between having her.' I jerked my head towards the nursery.

'She's wonderful,' Marianne said. 'I do think you're lucky. Don't be angry but I really do.'

The kettle screamed and I had to attend to it. Marianne didn't come in the kitchen. When I returned with the tray she was lighting a fresh cigarette.

'How's Malcolm?' she said.

'All right.'

'Oh good.' She looked happy.

'By which I mean just the same,' I said rather sharply. Marianne's eyes held mine for a moment and I got an odd impression of blankness, a kind of opaque density through which nothing penetrated, over which she had laid a thin social veneer.

'Isn't it any better?' she said with every appearance of concern, which I felt sure was genuine. Nevertheless she was not really there, somehow, in a way that puzzled me. She seemed to have herself under some kind of remote control.

'Worse,' I said. 'He's all adoring and dependent.'

She looked away. 'You'll have to be kind to him,' she said.

I felt this keenly, from her, and didn't know what to say that wouldn't reflect on her and David. Between us we seemed to form a pretty horrific pattern. Why not Marianne and Malcolm – two nice, ordinary, vulnerable people? Life was absurd.

'It's very difficult,' I said at last. I could not tell her I was going away.

'Yes, of course.' She drank from her cup, long eyelashes blackened and brushing her cheeks.

'Are things any better for you?' I attempted.

She put down the cup and smiled at me. 'No,' she said. 'I'm just the same too.'

I couldn't insult her by saying time would heal everything, the way people always reassure anyone nursing grief, although I thought it might. But, as if she guessed, Marianne went on, 'Nothing's going to be any different, Val. I know that. It's just one of those things.' The way she said it, it even sounded new and inexpressibly painful. Unnecessary to ask if she still loved David when her face and voice made it so clear; stupid to say he might come back when she obviously knew he wouldn't.

'I'm sorry,' I said, falling back on the only words we have when people we love are unhappy. Faced with Marianne, I cared greatly for her: her physical presence had always been strong, though she faded in absence. Looking at her now I remembered the girl I had defended years ago. The good old days, it seemed almost, when you could still help someone you loved by lashing out at those who hurt them.

'It's all right,' she said. 'I think I knew it would all end up like this one day. It was too good to last.'

This was hardly the way I would have described what little happiness she had had, but there was no point in arguing. 'I wish there was something I could do,' I said. 'Are you looking after yourself properly?'

'Oh yes,' she said vaguely. 'Don't worry about me.'

'But I do,' I said. 'Have you got another flat?'

She said, 'Yes,' and I could read nothing into it.

'Is it nice?'

'It's not bad.'

I felt slightly frantic now, suddenly. 'Have you gone back to modelling?' I asked and watched her closely, ashamed of myself.

There wasn't a flicker on her face. If I had not been told I would have suspected nothing. Perhaps after all Sally and her informants had been mistaken. Jealous wish-fulfilment, or genuine bad sight. 'I do some now and then,' Marianne said. 'Are you still studying a lot?'

'I was until recently.'

'Oh well, of course you can't now; you must be awfully busy.' Again what anyone else might have said, but from her inoffensive. 'Is she a good baby? Does she cry much?' She looked at me eagerly.

'I don't really know,' I said. 'I can't compare her with others. She has her good and bad days.'

'But you're coping all right?' An impressed tone of voice. I said, 'Yes.'

'Can I see her again before I go? I'll be very quiet.'

'Of course,' I said, 'but you're not going yet, are you?'

'Oh, I ought to,' she said vaguely. 'I've got things to do.'

We went back in the nursery. Vicky was awake but quiet. Marianne said, 'Hullo, Vicky,' very softly, as if afraid of disturbing her.

'Pick her up if you like,' I said. It had only just occurred to me that she might want to. I had always been embarrassed when people offered me their babies to hold.

'Don't you mind?' She looked disproportionately grateful.

'Why should I?'

Gingerly Marianne edged Vicky out of her cot and held her firm in both arms, close to her body.

'Careful she doesn't mess you up,' I said. 'She dribbles, quite apart from the other end. I usually wear an overall to deal with her.'

'It doesn't matter,' Marianne said. She rocked Vicky gently.

'She likes you,' I said, embarrassed.

'She's beautiful.' She spoke helplessly, the way you might say 'I love you' when there is no hope.

'Well, she's not as cross-eyed as she was,' I said, to change the atmosphere.

Marianne, luckily, took it up. 'Oh Val, she's not cross-eyed at all.'

'Well, she certainly was,' I said.

'Oh, they all are, aren't they?' She looked down at Vicky and said – the first really natural remark I had heard from her since she arrived; 'Oh Val, isn't it funny you having a baby?'

'It certainly is,' I said.

'I think it's all going to work out fine, though,' she added, 'in spite of everything. You know.'

It seemed I was not the only one afraid of speaking openly, so I just said, 'Yes. You're probably right.'

Marianne looked out of the window above Vicky's head. She was the only person I had seen who could cuddle and obviously adore a baby without talking rubbish to it. She said, 'It's so funny how we've both ended up,' as if the two of us had reached a final state, and then suddenly with great decision, 'I must go, Val. I'm sorry but I'll have to dash.' She made to return Vicky to her cot.

'Bring her down with you,' I said. 'She might as well go in the pram now it's stopped raining.'

We walked down the stairs, Marianne stepping carefully in her heels. Outside in the garden she put Vicky into the pram and I covered her up. Vicky made soft spluttering noises but appeared content.

'Do come again soon,' I said urgently.

'I'll phone you,' Marianne said. I looked at her with doubt. 'Oh I will, honest,' she said.

'Can I phone you?' I asked.

'No, you can't.' She hesitated. 'Not yet.'

'All right,' I said. We looked at each other. I wanted to hug her, but the moment wasn't right and she made no move. 'Take care of yourself,' I said inadequately.

She smiled at me. 'You mustn't worry about me,' she said.

I stood in the garden long after she had gone, although I was cold. 'Well,' I said to Vicky, 'somebody loves you.' She looked at me blankly, clasping and unclasping her hands. I felt a fool but Marianne had disturbed me. 'Oh, you'll be all right,' I told her. 'You've got a father and grandparents and an aunt and now Marianne as well. You're loaded.'

She just lay there, looking small and vacant. It was probably the first time I had simply looked at her, apart from doing things for her.

'I have to go,' I said.

THIRTY-SEVEN

In May the weather improved and Malcolm became energetic and full of plans. He was going to start studying again for his banking exams. He thought we should look at houses. He was wondering about the car again, whether we should face facts and sell it, or hang on and hope. I longed in a way to save him all this by saying, quite simply, why there was no need for it, but of course I couldn't. Our evenings now were very quiet. There was little money to go anywhere, though Jean was a willing baby-sitter, but sometimes we went for drives. The countryside was growing pretty again, cherry blossom falling everywhere and the leaves dancing. I thought sourly of all the young couples rushing off into the woods to get pregnant.

'When d'you have that examination?' Malcolm asked.

'Next week,' I said, and added, 'I thought you were counting the hours.'

He flushed. 'Well, you know. I wouldn't be human if I didn't want to ... get back to normal.' He paused. 'It'll be great, won't it? After all this time.'

It seemed a shame for him to get too excited. 'It may be a while before I'm back to normal,' I said. 'You don't get over having a baby just like that.'

'No, of course not,' he said. 'I know that.'

We had parked off the road at the top of a hill to look down on the surrounding woods. It was a view I had loved but it didn't seem the same. I had so much to think about and it brought back too many memories. In a way I would almost have liked to set fire to everything. I wondered how many others had gone for walks and drives and thought themselves too clever to get caught. Did they even think what getting caught really meant?

It was a long time since I had tried to talk to Malcolm, but knowing how little time I had left with him I thought I would try again. Partly it was curiosity, partly an urge to think aloud. There was also a dash of that idiotic urge to philosophize that you get from being high up.

'Are you happy?' I said.

He didn't answer at once. Then he said, 'What d'you mean?'

I shrugged. 'It couldn't be a simpler question.'

'I'm all right,' he said.

I thought, What the hell? and went on. 'Have you got what you wanted?'

He lit a dog-end. 'Well,' he said, 'I could do with a bit more money.'

'Oh, I know that,' I said. 'I mean the whole thing. Do you like working in a bank? You never talk about it.'

He looked surprised. 'Well, there's not much to say. I mean, what d'you want to know about it?'

'Well, do you like it?'

'It's all right.' He paused. 'It's a steady job; it has prospects. When I get these exams, for instance, we'll be a bit better off. The people are okay.'

'You don't wish you'd done something else?'

'Well, no. No, I don't think so.'

I looked at him. He needed a shave and that always gave him a rough, slightly gangsterish appearance. Alternatively, in a turban he could have posed for a sheik. Tall, dark and handsome: every girl's dream. Except mine.

'So you're happy in your work,' I said.

'I suppose so.' He looked uncertain, baffled.

'Is that all you want out of life?' I asked. 'A steady job?'

'Well,' he said reasonably, 'everybody needs one.'

'I know that.' I was annoyed. 'Don't you want anything else? Don't you feel you've missed anything?'

'It's different for me,' he said surprisingly. 'I never had the chance of going to college. You're bound to feel you've missed something.'

There was perception and lack of perception together: strange. I said, 'For how long? For ever, do you suppose?' and waited.

'I don't know,' Malcolm said. 'Maybe.'

'Oh. And that's all right, is it?'

'No.' He threw away the cigarette stub. 'But it can't be helped either.'

'It's hardly the same thing,' I said.

'Of course it isn't. You've had to give up more than I have. That's why it's tougher on you than me.'

'So you're quite happy?'

He didn't answer at once. Finally he said, 'Yeah. I'm all right.'

'That's not what I asked.' I became vehement. 'Do you like being married? Do you like being Vicky's father? Do you like being tied down? Are you happy, positively, actively *happy*?' Without raising my voice I was, in effect, shouting at him.

He looked at me with a mixed expression: surprise, indignation, patience. 'No one ever is,' he said at length.

'Why the hell not?' This time I did really shout.

He shook his head. 'Life isn't like that.'

'Well, why isn't it? And if it isn't, why can't you make it like that? Why should you give in to it all the time?'

'Who's giving in?' He frowned at my words and smiled to humour me. 'What are you on about?'

I thought now that maybe I was doing him a favour: that he could remember this conversation when I had gone and it might explain more than a letter. 'If you don't get what you want out of life,' I said, 'then you're giving in to it. You're letting it beat you.'

'No,' Malcolm said. 'You're just facing facts. You can't have everything you want.'

'But *why* not? *Why* can't you?'

'Well ...' He gestured vaguely, stuck for an answer. 'It just doesn't work out like that.'

'But it could,' I insisted. 'If you made it.'

'No.' He was positive but unmoved. We might have been discussing gravity.

'All right,' I said, breathing deeply to calm myself. 'So you think no one ever gets all they want. Right? So no one is ever really happy. Is that what you think?'

He looked away. 'Well, what d'you mean by happy?'

'Oh, good Lord, isn't it obvious?'

'I don't know, Val. I mean, everyone has good times and bad times, and things go up and down and you just make the best of them.'

'That's your philosophy?' I asked.

He hesitated. 'I suppose so.'

'You just make the best of things instead of trying to change them,' I said.

'You can't change everything,' he said patiently.

'But you might if you really tried.' I had to give him a final chance. 'Didn't you ever feel you were all-powerful, that you could do anything you wanted to?'

'Oh well,' he said, 'all kids feel like that.'

'That's all you think it is?'

'I don't know, Val. I suppose so.'

'Look,' I said. 'If you could have anything you wanted, what would you do? Be single again? Change me? Be rich? What?'

'What's the point?' He looked at me almost coldly, trapped.

'I want to know.'

'Well, I can't tell you.'

'Well, try.'

People walking past glanced curiously at the car. I waited. Malcolm looked sullen.

'Sure, I'd like more money,' he said. 'Who wouldn't?'

'And?' I prompted.

He grinned at me suddenly, disconcertingly. 'And you do have your off days. But I can't really picture being single again and not having you and Vicky, now she's here. Satisfied?'

I sank back in my seat, utterly tired and vanquished. I felt very cold. 'Oh yes,' I said. 'Completely.'

THIRTY-EIGHT

I looked out a suitcase. I thought what clothes to take. I checked on the times of trains. But I didn't go. It was rather like waiting to get up. You keep picturing yourself flinging off the bedclothes and leaping out of bed. You even see yourself washed and dressed, eating breakfast and leaving the house. Meanwhile you don't move; you lie warm and still.

I had my post-natal check up and was pronounced fit. I had contraceptive advice, too, though I had not planned on staying long enough to need it. It was suggested in a very down-to-earth way by my mother. Malcolm thought it an excellent idea since we had never been really sure how Vicky occurred. So I practised with a cap that flew out of my hand when laden with cream and landed sticky side down, like buttered toast, on the floor.

I decided to stay for Jean's birthday, which meant I would have to let Malcolm make love to me. Mentally I felt only distaste, but my body was tense and nervous. Malcolm kept saying, 'I won't hurt you, I won't hurt you,' but he did. Then he stopped and said, 'We don't have to do this, you know,' and I said, 'Don't be silly,' and tried to relax. He was a little too far gone really to change his mind but he was trying, I suppose, to show consideration. In the middle of it all Vicky yowled. Malcolm went on a little, then stopped as the volume mounted.

'Should you go in?' he asked in a voice heavy with disappointment.

'She must be all right,' I said. If it had to happen we might as well get it over. 'She was fed and changed an hour ago.'

But the noise continued and his mood was broken. He withdrew and lay down on his back. 'You'd better go and see,' he said. 'Or shall I go?'

'Oh, I'll go,' I said.

As I switched on the nursery light the bulb clicked and died. I swore softly and felt for Vicky. She was still crying, but when I lifted her out of the cot she stopped. I carried out a routine inspection. 'Well, you're dry,' I said to her. 'And you can't be hungry; you had a huge feed.' I put her back in the cot and the thin wail started again. It puzzled me because she was not used to being spoilt and picked up, especially at night. I shut the door so that Malcolm, if his condition allowed, might go to sleep. I felt odd, alone with Vicky in a dark room.

'Oh come on,' I said to her. 'Do shut up.' But she went on whimpering, a feeble yet penetrating noise. I rocked the cot a bit and poked at her with a finger. She grabbed the finger and hung on tightly. I had noticed before with surprise what a strong grip she had.

'You're all right, aren't you?' I said. 'Silly thing, you're all right.'

She stopped crying. The silence was blissful and miraculous; the future uncertain. 'Oh look,' I said, somehow the darkness making it all right to think aloud to her, 'I can't stay here all night, can I? Be reasonable. If you're trying to save me from a fate worse than death you're much too late.'

I tried to detach my finger and her grip tightened. I pulled myself free and she howled. I had a clear choice between returning to bed and Malcolm, and picking her up. I picked her up. Again the crying ceased. 'If this is your new game,' I said, 'I don't think much of it.' She clucked placidly to herself. 'Anyway,' I added, 'you'll have to do without me soon. It's a hard world, kid; you'll have to get tough.' I stood by the window and rocked her, looking out. The moon was up and a wind was swaying the trees. 'That's where I should be,' I said. 'Out there. Away. I'm not staying long, you know.

I can't. You picked the wrong mother, that's all.' Suddenly I wished I could explain to her, make her understand, which was ridiculous. I could not even make Malcolm understand. In fact there was no one I could talk to. Except Vicky, of course: the final irony. I wondered how they would explain to her when the time came. Would they blacken my character? Doubtless; there was no other way.

Soon, I thought, soon, watching the trees. I should have gone before. I don't know why I didn't. I could have seen a doctor anywhere. I'm bound to miss Jean's birthday some time. God, I must be crazy. Why am I still here? So easy, just to pack and get on a train. I must go soon.

I put Vicky back very carefully in her cot and let her hold a finger. I sat on a chair beside her, my hand hanging in the cot. She was quiet. Everything was quiet. I might have been alone in the world, just me and the baby clinging to my hand. It was pretty dreary being a baby, come to think of it. Whatever you wanted you could only yell and hope for the best. You lay in your filthy nappies, all wet and smelly, till someone came and replaced them with dry ones, and cleaned you up. You sucked away at milk formula and as like as not threw it up again all over yourself. People cooed at you when you were tired and left you alone when you were wide awake. You just lay there and stared at the ceiling or the sky or the beads on your pram or cot, and at the dark when it was night. Perhaps you were frightened. Maybe that was it. Perhaps you thought no one would ever come back and you'd be left alone in the dark for ever. Maybe it was like being unborn again, in a warm, dark world by yourself with that fight to get out still ahead.

The grip on my finger wasn't tight any more. I took away my hand and there was silence. I was free; I could go. But I didn't move. I just sat there, quite still, and started to cry.

THIRTY-NINE

I made Jean a birthday cake and bought her a record and she and my mother came round for the evening. It was a good party. Jean and Malcolm danced and my mother and I watched them. They looked good together; Jean was growing up fast. I hoped she would be luckier than I had been.

My mother said, 'Are you all right? You look tired.'

I said, 'I am, rather.' I felt jumpy, unsettled.

'Has she been keeping you awake?' my mother asked.

'A bit,' I said.

'They all do at times,' she assured me. 'She'll get over it.'

I couldn't talk to her any more, though I loved her as much as ever and she was the same. The barrier was inside me. It seemed I had lost what I had sacrificed so much to preserve: our closeness and understanding. So we talked about things that did not matter. If I had tried to explain I would have sounded like a Method actor playing an American adolescent in a bad film. ('Gee, Mom, I'm all mixed up. Like I mean, gee, I don't know,' and all that.) Given such an alternative, anyone would have kept quiet. And it was not as if she could help me.

Malcolm and I had painful intercourse. So much so that he suggested I should have another examination. I did. I was assured that I was back to normal but I couldn't expect not to be a little sore at first. I should use plenty of cream and relax. I wasn't worried, was I? Worry could make me tense. I must relax and have confidence in the method. I said no, I wasn't worried. I went home and told Malcolm they had advised me not to overdo it. He was disappointed but concerned, and left me alone more, restricting himself to once a week, and that with a mixture of urgency and guilt. I felt ashamed but also relieved; it suited me much better. Maybe I was curtailing his only pleasure, but what pleasure did I have? It now seemed fantastic in the true sense of the word that I had ever found this a pleasure. I understood all I had ever read about women being pestered. It was obscene to go through a charade of giving yourself when you felt nothing physically except pain and nothing emotionally but detachment. It was simple rape and I was amazed that Malcolm did not appear to recognize it as such. I felt I was a corpse being used, like the idea I had always had that Othello meant to make love to Desdemona when she was dead.

I slept badly, half-listening for Vicky, although she seldom cried now in the night. I dreamed things I could hardly remember but which I knew were unpleasant and left me unrested and heavily depressed. Once I had a real nightmare and woke up in the middle, terrified, my face damp with sweat. I had been in a deep pit, trying to climb up the sides, but they were rocky and full of gravel and hurt my hands. I went on struggling but as I neared the top I found it wasn't the top; I had made hardly any progress at all. Mrs Franklin peered over the edge, looking terribly cross.

Malcolm studied in the evenings, every evening. He found it heavy going; he kept sighing and looking round, and he hadn't enough cigarettes to help him. We lived on stew and bacon and eggs, and when I bought vegetables they were always ones that took ages to prepare and cook because those were the cheap ones. I had soup and things on toast for lunch and spooned cereal and orange juice into Vicky. She spat out the cereal – on to her bib if I was lucky – but guzzled the orange juice like an alcoholic.

It was hot in June and people said we were getting all our summer over in one go, just as they say if we have a mild winter that we'll suffer for it later on. It's strange that mere weather can evoke such a fierce moral sense. It's almost as if they want to be punished. Perhaps Malcolm is right and it's just that, like him, they expect very little out of life. I pushed Vicky's pram round the shops and tried to keep clear of strangers who wanted to talk to her or touch her. I had a strong feeling of unreality: this couldn't be me involved in this endless, repetitive routine. I half-expected something to happen, like an explosion, when I knew in fact that action could only come from me. I rationalized my state into a waiting period until Vicky was older. I had planned for too early a date, that was all; absurd to panic. But when I looked at her and especially when she smiled at me (though I knew it was probably just wind) I felt like a traitor – someone stroking a dog he knows he is going to shoot.

FORTY

MALCOLM arrived home in a state of great excitement. 'Come on, get your coat. We're going to see a house.'

I was jolted out of my apathy. 'What house? Where?'

'About two miles nearer home.' He still called the village home. 'Look, this is it.' He thrust the agent's blurb into my hands. 'You can read it in the car. Come on, love; get your coat.'

I gestured at Vicky, who was on the couch. 'What about her?'

'Oh, bring her along.'

'Won't they mind?'

'Who?' He stared at me.

'Well, the owners of course.'

'No, it's empty. Okay?' He dumped Vicky in her carry-cot and grabbed the handles.

'Don't throw her about,' I said.

'I didn't.' He looked surprised.

'And I don't need a coat,' I said.

We drove fast. So much sudden, rapid movement made me almost physically dizzy. It was hard to read the print. 'Modernized terrace house, needs decoration . . . two cosy reception rooms . . . kitchen and W. C. . . . two sunny bedrooms . . .'

'They can't be sunny all the time,' I said.

'What?'

'The bedrooms. It says two sunny bedrooms.'

'Oh well.' He shrugged slightly. 'You know what house agents are like.'

'I know what "modernized" means too,' I said. 'Have you

forgotten some of those flats? And "needs decoration". That'll be plaster falling gently into the soup plates.'

He didn't answer. When we reached the road we coasted slowly down it looking for the number. It wasn't needed. The luxuriant growth of weeds and hedge in the front garden was sufficient identification. Malcolm stopped the car. 'I suppose this is it,' he said.

'You bet it is,' I said. We both sat and looked at it.

'It's been empty a while,' Malcolm said. 'That's why it's going cheap. Well, comparatively cheap.'

'You mean that's one reason,' I said.

Malcolm took a deep breath. 'Val, there's no point in hating it on sight.'

'Why not?' I said. 'We don't have to have it, do we?'

'We have to have something,' he said rather loudly. 'That rent is crippling us.'

'D'you think I haven't noticed?'

In the back seat Vicky, disturbed by our shouting, began to cry.

'Oh God,' said Malcolm, 'now she's off.'

Something burned inside me. 'It's hardly surprising,' I said.

He looked genuinely puzzled. 'What d'you mean?'

'She doesn't like us fighting,' I said.

'We're not fighting.'

I wondered if I was going mad, I felt so violent.

'Come on,' said Malcolm gently. 'We'd better look at it now we're here.'

We got out of the car and each took one handle of the carry-cot, a ridiculous symbol of non-existent unity. The front gate creaked and stuck; I took charge of the wailing baby while Malcolm pushed. 'Right,' he said, 'in you go.'

The garden was full of the feathery purple plant that always seems to thrive on neglect. We brushed past it and Malcolm put the key in the front door. It opened easily. 'Well done,' I said.

We stepped into a microscopic hall and almost mounted the

stairs in one movement. The kitchen door hung open ahead of us and a blackened gas stove was visible.

'They've left a cooker,' Malcolm said.

'Is that what you call it?' I walked past him with Vicky and into the room. 'They've left a bath, too,' I said, 'and who can blame them?'

'But you never –' he began, and then, 'In the *kitchen?*' He caught up with me and looked. It was tiny, with a lid covered with fablon. Inside there was a kind of ledge. 'Oh, a sitz bath,' Malcolm said.

'In the kitchen,' I said. 'Where else?' I swung the carry-cot a little; Vicky was still crying. 'That means no bathroom,' I said loudly. 'Do you realize that means no bathroom? Did you read this thing?' I pulled the agent's sheet from my pocket. ' "Two sunny bedrooms". That's the sum total of the delights upstairs.'

Malcolm let the lid fall and leaned on it. 'Can't you shut her up?' he said. He had never complained like this before.

'No, I can't,' I said, 'She's hungry. She was due to be fed when you dragged us off here.'

He sighed and shut his eyes for a moment. 'Well, you should've said.'

I walked out of the kitchen and into one of the cosy reception rooms. Malcolm followed me. The room was small with faded wallpaper covered in flowers, and cream paint. Malcolm looked around. 'No sign of damp,' he said cheerfully.

I was standing by the window, which gave a good view of the back yard, coal bunker, dustbin and – 'What's that shed?' I said suddenly.

Malcolm joined me at the window. 'I don't know.'

'It's the lavatory,' I said. I consulted the paper again. ' "Kitchen and W.C." My God, they're modest. They missed a chance there. Why not "convenient lavatory with healthy open-air aspect"? My God, why not?' I was shaking. Vicky's screams increased. I seized her out of the carry-cot and held her to me, but only for a moment. 'Oh Christ,' I said in despair, 'she's soaking.' The cries ceased and she gurgled happily.

'She doesn't seem to mind,' said Malcolm with relief. 'At least she's stopped crying.'

'Well, I mind,' I said sharply. My eyes were burning. I had not realized I wanted to cry.

'Come on,' said Malcolm. 'Let's just have a quick look at the rest of it.'

Returned to the cot, Vicky howled afresh.

'You'll have to carry her,' Malcolm said. 'I can't stand that row.'

'Well, I'm not enjoying it,' I said, 'but you can't blame her for crying when she's soaking wet.'

'I'm not blaming her,' he said. We looked at each other and I was the first to break. 'But she's quiet if you carry her, wet or not,' he added.

'All right,' I said, picking her up, 'so it doesn't matter if I get soaked.'

'You could put the blanket round her.'

'And ruin a perfectly good blanket?'

'Well, you can wash it, can't you?'

'Oh yes,' I said. 'I just love washing blankets. I don't know why anyone bothers with machines when they can have so much fun washing blankets by hand.'

'Well, then, send it to the laundry. Burn the damn thing –' He was suddenly shouting. 'For God's sake, Val, does it matter for once?'

We were both quiet. Vicky was quiet. An ominous, electric silence took over the room. Very slowly and ostentatiously I took the blanket out of the cot and wrapped it round Vicky.

We inspected the rest of the house in the same silence. Our feet echoed on the bare boards as we walked about. In the other reception room there was a fireplace full of rubbish and a bay window overlooking the choked garden. Upstairs the two bedrooms were simply two bedrooms. There was nothing anyone could have said about them. We walked downstairs and out through the kitchen door. A cat fled away from the dustbin. Malcolm disappeared into the lavatory shed and I was left for a moment alone in the yard holding Vicky, now peacefully asleep in her damp blanket.

There was a gush of water and Malcolm emerged. 'Well, it works,' he said, the first words we had spoken for about ten minutes.

I said, 'Good,' and turned away.

FORTY-ONE

'I know it's not much,' Malcolm said. We were in bed at last after a long evening of frosty politeness and television. 'But it's a start. We can afford it. We could do it up and sell it in a few years and get something quite nice. It would just give us a chance to get on our feet.'

He was planning my life away, so sure I would be there. Why didn't I just say, 'I'm leaving you. I'm leaving Vicky. You won't need a house?' Why, and this was more to the point, had I not gone already?

He sighed heavily and turned half away, thinking no doubt that I was still sulking. I knew it had cost him something to make the first move, so I had to speak. 'I know,' I said.

'It won't always be like this.' He went on speaking in the same reasonable way. 'I'll get rises. We won't always be so hard up. When Vicky's older you can get a job if you like.'

He was giving me his kind permission and thereby making it clear that for the moment I was a prisoner. But why, if I meant to leave her, did I always take her with me when I went shopping? She would be alone in the house when I caught the train.

'Yes, I could,' I said.

'Things are never as bad as you expect,' he continued. 'I mean, you thought you'd hate Vicky, you didn't want her. Well, neither of us did, but now you're marvellous with her.' He paused, pleased with the analogy.

'She's not much trouble,' I said slowly.

'There you are.' A faintly triumphant note. 'And you hate the house now. Well, I don't like it much either, but you imagine it when we've painted it. A few coats of paint will make quite a difference.'

He made it sound easy to fix. It was a pity that people could not be painted.

'And look,' he said, as I didn't reply, 'maybe we can do something about a bathroom. We could make the kitchen into a proper bathroom with a toilet and have a kitchen-diner next door. Or we could convert one of the bedrooms and sleep downstairs. We don't *need* four rooms. We've managed all right in three.'

'That's true,' I said, as he seemed to prefer me to answer.

'You can get council grants, I think,' he said hopefully. 'Honestly, Val, it won't be so bad. We can work on it. It might even be fun, seeing how much we can change it.'

'Can I think it over?' I asked, with the old trapped feeling. It was like getting married all over again: good-bye special person, university, the unknown challenge. Again you had to crush your own character, to crucify yourself. Was it a fair punishment for having once – so long ago, it seemed now – enjoyed making love?

'Sure, you think it over,' Malcolm said, 'but don't take too long.'

'It won't disappear,' I said.

'No, I suppose not.' He hesitated. 'Friends again?'

What else could I say? 'Yes, friends.'

'Oh Val.' With what seemed like enormous relief he turned over, putting his arm round me. 'Love. I'm sorry you've had a rough time. It's going to be better, I promise.' He started kissing my shoulder, my neck. I felt the warmth drain from my body. Suddenly he stopped. 'You don't want to, do you?' he said. 'It's not the same for you. It hasn't been the same since Vicky was born.'

Confronted with near-truth, I panicked. 'It still hurts,' I said. 'I'm frightened.'

'I'm sorry,' he said. 'Is that really all it is? I've been wondering.'

I couldn't deal the ultimate insult. No one deserved that, and I could hear the tension in his voice. 'That's all it is,' I said. 'Did you think I'd gone off you or something?'

'Something like that.' He spoke more easily already. 'Well, you know. I couldn't help noticing.'

'Well, you can stop worrying,' I said, wanting to kill the subject. 'You just try having a baby and see how sexy you feel.'

He laughed, mainly with relief. 'Okay, I'll remember that. Only I'd hate you to go cold on me. Such a waste of talent. And I don't feel a bit cold about you.' His hand lingered over my breast, then withdrew. I could feel his reluctance. 'Okay,' he said, 'we've got plenty of time. So long as we get back to our old high standard eventually. Because, in case you've forgotten, we used to be a pretty high-powered couple.'

'I haven't forgotten,' I said.

FORTY-TWO

It was hot. I sat in the garden and watched Vicky, naked except for her nappy, on a rug. I tried to read but I hardly saw the print. I was swamped by the effort of trying to think clearly.

She was fit and healthy and mostly cheerful. All ready, in fact, to be transferred to Mrs Ross. She would be well cared for, I knew. What harm did the occasional *Watchicoo* really do? I would not be there to be irritated by it.

I would not be there. I focussed on Vicky. I would not see her grow beyond this age. For me she would always be this size. As for her, she would not remember me at all. If she had been adopted she would not have known me. It was just the same. I had only made it more difficult by waiting.

And yet, would Mrs Ross, for all her fuss in the daytime, get up in the night if she cried and really needed someone? Would she be left alone in the dark when she was frightened? But I didn't want to live in that house; I didn't want Vicky to live in that house. Why did I feel so responsible? I wasn't sloppy about her; I hadn't wallowed in motherhood like other women.

Would I feel better if my mother could have her? But my mother couldn't have her, so the question was irrelevant. She was too young to notice whom she was with in any case, so what was I worrying about?

'Honestly, you'd be better off,' I said to Vicky. She grinned at me toothlessly; she had the sort of cheerfulness that you get from a dog. You can even insult it and it will wag its tail so long as you insult it in a pleasant voice. 'You horrible, stinking dog,' you can say, and it wags itself into a frenzy of pleasure as it hears your sugary voice. But I didn't want to say anything like that to Vicky. She was improving all the time; she had nothing else to do. It was very unfair, I thought. It would have been so easy to leave the wrinkled, misshapen, discoloured object I had given birth to.

I went indoors and got orange juice and spooned some of it into Vicky's mouth. She took it greedily. I thought how necessarily helpless and trusting she was. I might be poisoning her for all she knew.

I returned to the deck-chair. It was lovely to be thin again, lovely to sunbathe, lovely not to be ashamed of my body. No more children, ever. One was enough, more than enough, in fact. 'You're more than enough,' I said to Vicky and she shoved a fist in her mouth and looked coy. I pulled at a corner of the rug to draw her further into the shade. She was probably too young to cook herself, as I intended to.

Upstairs, as if in another world, the telephone rang for the second time that afternoon. I ignored it. I knew from experience that if I ran all the way it would stop when I laid my hand on it. Once I knew I was not going to move, it merely contributed to my comfort. It was the summer equivalent of being warm and dry in the house while the rain pours down outside. Then it suddenly occurred to me that it might be Marianne and worth running for. I jumped up, with the heavy effort always required after sunbathing, and moved a few paces irresolutely, half-hurrying. True to form, the ringing stopped. I sank down. If it was Marianne she would have to ring again; I promised her mentally I would get up at once. *Moll Flanders*, which Malcolm had once confused with *Fanny Hill* until I disillusioned him, lay on the grass beside me, its jacket buckling in the sun. I pushed it under my chair. There was no point in trying to read. I needed action. Malcolm would soon be pressing for a decision: to get his bank loan, to buy the house, to sell the car, no doubt. What was I doing here? The door of the jail was unlocked.

I lit a cigarette as a substitute for action and wondered what percentage of tobacco sales came from irresolute people. I didn't like myself in this state at all. But the sun induced euphoria: if I closed my eyes I could float away.

Dozing or daydreaming, I lost count of time, but I jumped when the garden gate clicked. There were rapid footsteps on the path. I opened my eyes and saw Malcolm. 'Hullo,' I said, 'you're early.' I could not see his face very clearly.

He stood still, abruptly, on the edge of the grass. 'You didn't answer the phone,' he said, and his voice sounded odd.

I was relieved. 'Oh, it was you, was it? I'm sorry but I can never catch it in time. Does it matter?'

'It was Sally,' he said. He still sounded strained, as if tight in the throat. I was alarmed without knowing why. 'Val, I'm sorry, I've got an awful shock for you; you'd better brace yourself. It's Marianne. She's dead.'

I just looked at him. I couldn't speak. Pointlessly I took my sunglasses off and the sun nearly blinded me. I opened my mouth and no sound came out. But I felt nothing. His words conveyed nothing; they made no sense.

'Oh love, I'm sorry,' he said. I went on making what seemed like a colossal effort to speak without any result. 'I know how fond you were of her,' he went on. 'It's a terrible shock for you. Sally was pretty shaken, too. She said she never imagined this could happen to someone she went to school with. She wanted me to tell you in case you saw the papers.'

He came nearer; he held out his hands and knelt on the grass beside me. Without knowing I was going to speak I heard myself say, 'But what *happened*?' in quite a normal voice.

He took my hands and squeezed them hard. His were hot and sticky. He said, 'Val, I'm sorry. She killed herself. It's – in the papers. Her – her parents have been to identify her – oh, God, I'm sorry but you'd have to know some time.'

'Killed herself?' My voice came from nowhere.

'Yes. Last night. They're trying to trace her mother.'

FORTY-THREE

I became hysterical and Malcolm had to slap me. When I was quiet he carried me indoors. I lay on the couch and he drew the curtains. He moved around very softly as though I was ill and brought me hot, sweet tea. I drank it and was promptly sick. He cleared up and stood by the window until I asked him, politely, to go away.

The room was cool after the garden. I lay on my side and clung to a cushion. I think I tore it; I found a great rent in it later. The tears just streamed from my eyes, down my face, over my nose, into the cushion. The room was full of the noise of my sobbing, animal noises, like being in labour. I had to take great gulps of air through my mouth; I felt I was choking.

Then it stopped. Was that all I could do? Was that all a life meant to me, Marianne's life? I was shivering. Malcolm opened the door.

'Would you like a cigarette?' he said. I didn't answer, so he lit two and placed one in my mouth. When I put my fingers to it, my hand shook like someone with Parkinson's disease. Malcolm gave me a handkerchief and I wiped my face and blew my nose.

'Can I get you anything?' he said with great tenderness. I struggled to sit up, but it was difficult and he had to help me.

'What did she do?' I said.

'Oh Val –' The question seemed to upset him.

'I want to know,' I said. 'I'm quite calm now. You can tell me. You've got to tell me.'

He looked at me fixedly as if he couldn't look anywhere else. He said, 'Gas. It won't have hurt. I promise.'

After a long time I said, 'Have you got a paper? I want to see a paper.'

Malcolm said, 'No. I – didn't think.' I said nothing. He added with difficulty, 'Do you want me to get one?'

I said, 'Yes.' I think I still felt it might not be true.

'But I don't like to leave you.'

'I'm all right,' I said.

When he had gone it didn't seem true at all.

FORTY-FOUR

WE moved into the house last month, but there is still a great deal to be done. Malcolm talks of being finished in time for our wedding anniversary, but I don't think it's likely. He has worked very hard, first in the garden scything all the vegetation to near ground level, and then in the house clearing up after the workmen. The alterations are quite successful.

He got a good price for the car and we bought a lot of second-hand furniture. It's jammed in the two rooms upstairs at the moment, most of it anyway; we more or less live in one room downstairs as the rest of the place is in such a mess. We had to move as soon as we could, because of the rent and the bank loan. I suppose we shall find it cheaper living here, well, I know we shall, but right now it's hard to tell because we keep buying paint and material for curtains. My poor mother is going to make them. Jean is very excited and it's all we can do to make sure she finishes her homework before coming round to paint. When the workmen were here she was on holiday and always under their feet. She thinks it's wonderful that we've got a home of our own.

I don't mind the painting; in fact it's quite restful, being such a mechanical job. We let Jean do base coats only as she's enthusiastic rather than expert, but I think she enjoys it more, anyway, because she can see what she's covering up. Sometimes Jeff and Christine come round – she's better than Carol but not as nice as Marie – and there are five of us at it, but then it usually degenerates into a party, with records and beer.

Malcolm took his holiday as soon as we moved in, but that's over now, of course, so his evenings are very full. He's got exams next month and has to study as well as paint. I do my share. But it's no more James Bond for him or television at the moment. He doesn't seem to mind. He looks a bit tired sometimes but he's very cheerful. He likes the house; he thinks it's all worthwhile. He's even started making jokes again and putting on funny voices.

In the daytime it's very quiet here. The children next door are at school and on the other side there is only an elderly couple. They've been here all their married life. I suppose lots of people do that, live in one place for years on end, and think nothing of it.

Autumn is coming early this year. Already the leaves are turning yellow and some are falling. It used to be my favourite season, but last year I hardly noticed it, having other things to think about. This year it means I must hurry, make up my mind, because night school courses start soon. I haven't quite decided yet. If I do a degree course it will probably take five years. That means I could be qualified to teach when Vicky starts school. It seems a long time, but to get what you want you have to plan ahead. On the other hand, if I take a commercial course I could get a job next year, in theory, if I sent Vicky to a nursery. Only I don't want to do that. She's grown such a lot I can hardly believe it. She can sit up now, if I prop her up with cushions, and she's so interesting and alive. I can't take a daytime job; I would miss so much. I could work in the evenings, though, as a waitress maybe, they say the tips are good, and do a postal degree. I wonder how long that would take; I must find out. There's so much to check up on; I've let that stupid painting interfere.

Whatever I do will take a long time, so I'm certainly here for years. Maybe if I really worked flat out I could do a degree course in less than five years. They say it's not possible, but I think it all depends on how much you want to. I've thought about everything. I've no idea if I shall be a good teacher, but it's the only job that will give me free time and enough money to support us both. Meanwhile we can manage here. I've been too impatient; I must learn to wait. I can't take her now. It wouldn't be fair. We'd be separated all day and I couldn't earn enough. No, I've got to get something out of this. I can stand it, knowing it's not for ever. It's my best chance now of getting what I want. I must realize this will take time. It's unfortunate, but it can't be avoided. There's too much at stake.

Mrs Franklin never wrote again. She still has my last lot of work, too. So it's no good expecting help from her. Always better to rely on yourself really. I should have known. I've put myself on a nineteenth-century course, with some reluctance because the sentimentality makes me cringe, but at the same time they write so well. Dickens, for instance : those superb scenes that jerk your tears even while you contemptuously dismiss them as tear-jerkers. Will I ever be untouched by Peggoty's account of Mrs Copperfield's last hours? I read it first when I was twelve, in Lyons of all places, and the tears streamed down my face. But I can't read *Wuthering Heights* any more. That's another kind of weeping and it scares me.

Malcolm seems surprised that I'm working again. Though he went on talking about it as a possibility, it appears he never really thought I would. But he doesn't object so long as I keep him happy. He's rather like Vicky in a way, only less rewarding. He needs food, warmth, sleep and love. I've learnt to do quite a good job in facsimile love. Oh, I know I always despised pretence, but, really, what alternative is there? If he gets sour he can object to so much, my degree course, my attention to Vicky in particular, and after all we do depend entirely on his money, such as it is. For the moment, at any rate. Experiencing this dependence of woman on man has been a giant lesson to me; I swear Vicky will not have to learn it. I'm going to see that she's independent and that nothing cuts across her life as it has across mine. She's going to have a real marriage and a real career – everything she wants, no less. But to get this for her I must be patient and, for a while, subservient. So I minister to all Malcolm's needs with a show of pleasure. I've made him very happy; he's so pleased I enjoy sex again – God! But if it keeps him sweet and hardworking it's worth it. All a question of priority really. There's Vicky to provide for, and our future together.

I'm not sure when I first realized I couldn't leave her, that the whole plan was absurd from the start. She grows more absorbing every day, so there's every reason now why I should want to be with her. That awful day put the lid on my departure, I suppose, but before that the night in the nursery took its toll and earlier that visit did something. I don't know; I've tried to pin it down. Not that it matters, but I find it interesting. I don't like to be a mystery to myself. Sometimes I think it began in the hospital when I chose her name, although that seems ridiculous.

That day, that visit: why do I find it so hard to say Marianne's name? I could cry now just thinking about her, helplessly like a child. It hurt so much to read the paper and yet I had to; and it took so long to stop seeing it, the print word for word in my head. It was a nasty paper, so what could I expect? But the words still haunt me. They made it sound so sensational with their gas-filled room in the notorious red-light district, and all that. Did they have to say a convicted prostitute? No one had to know that; it's absurd. They can't understand.

She left no letters to anyone. I was appalled at my own selfishness in expecting one. Even in death you want your friend to think of you, to explain, even to comfort in advance. It shocks me. 'You mustn't worry about me,' she said when I last saw her. That's all I have.

They never succeeded in tracing her mother. Wherever she is, with her commercial traveller or someone else or maybe alone, she will never know. She is a middle-aged woman and she has a daughter who is dead but she doesn't know. She probably thinks she's all right, if she ever thinks of her at all, that is, after so many years. It's no good; I must stop thinking about it. I want to scream and cry. There is nothing I can do that will help; was there ever anything? We are all alone in the end; Marianne took her own way out and I must take mine. But it's hard to be strong all the time : I need someone to believe in me, to reassure me, someone I can talk to. Because sometimes, when I'm tired or depressed, the fear comes; suppose I never get away? And I don't know how to fight it alone. I wish Vicky could understand what it's all about.

Vicky. I wake her up, feed her and change her. I cuddle her warm little body. We have a lot to do, so we'd better get busy. I fix her securely in a fortress of cushions and she watches me as I wash up. I spent the morning with Dickens while she slept, then we played after lunch. We must go shopping now for the meal tonight and then to the library to change my books. I try to be quick, but she's very good there and doesn't cry while she waits. I wrap her up well in the pram and we walk down the road. The pram crunches over the leaves. It's a crisp sort of day and the air is invigorating. Every hour brings it nearer, that's the way I must look at it. I've got to be strong.

'One day,' I say to Vicky, 'we're going away, you and I,' and she looks at me and laughs.